Fic Bro
Brown, Carolyn.

Evening star

EVENING STAR

A Drifters and Dreamers Romance

EVENING STAR

•

Carolyn Brown

AVALON BOOKS
NEW YORK

Published by Thomas Bouregy & Co., Inc.
160 Madison Avenue, New York, NY 10016

Library of Congress Cataloging-in-Publication Data

Brown, Carolyn, 1948–
    Evening star / Carolyn Brown.
        p. cm.
    ISBN 978-0-8034-9866-2 (acid-free paper)
    I. Title.

    PS3552.R685275E74   2007
    813'.54—dc22   2007025770

PRINTED IN THE UNITED STATES OF AMERICA
ON ACID-FREE PAPER
BY HADDON CRAFTSMEN, BLOOMSBURG, PENNSYLVANIA

This one is for Todd Morgan.

Chapter One

Addison Carter had never been so humiliated or downright mad in her entire life. Her father and brother had said she'd never be accepted as a female doctor and she'd proved them wrong—at least for three days. Now she had to get back on that train and retrace her journey from Healdton, Oklahoma to eastern Arkansas. Eat crow and wash it down with pride. If she could find a hole she'd gladly crawl in it and die.

"No, they won't win," she muttered under her breath and drew her coat closer against the bitter cold north wind whistling down Main Street, kicking up red dust devils along the way. "No one is taking my pride."

Besides, embarrassment couldn't even come in second in the race with plain old mad. She could have chewed up Magnolia Oil executives and spit pieces of

1

their sneers from Oklahoma to the Pacific Ocean. She'd survive. Neither her family nor anyone in Arkansas would ever know she'd been sent packing just because she was a woman. She'd enlist in the service as a nurse and go overseas first. Her training exceeded that of a nurse so they'd be glad to get her. She eyed the new black leather satchel at her feet, a present from her brother when Magnolia Oil Company sent her the contract and the letter. No, they didn't need to meet Addison Carter. They'd seen the school records, read the many letters of recommendation from the professors. They'd hire her without an interview. After all, women were named Sue or Edna, not Addison. That name was reserved in the holy courts of heaven for the male gender.

Euphoria lasted until she arrived at the Magnolia Oil Company office where the driver who'd met her at the train station in Ardmore ushered her in with a big grin on his face. When the officers of the company looked up from behind a massive mahogany desk, their faces registered nothing less than pure shock. Addison Carter was a woman. Great God, they couldn't have hired a woman. Addison was a man's name. What was she doing with a man's name? When the sputtering stopped, the driver said he'd take her back to Ardmore to catch the next eastbound train. They put their heads together and decided that they'd put her up in the Hotel Ardmore until the next morning, since it was their mistake. One of the men was going to Ardmore after five o'clock that evening. Surely she could entertain herself in Healdton for three hours. According to them, it was senseless to make an extra trip to Ardmore just to return her.

"Might bankrupt the whole damn company," she swore, pushing a strand of kinky, curly red hair out of her face. Two trunks and her bags sat beside a bench in front of the drug store. She'd plopped down on the bench, determined that she'd seen all of Healdton, Oklahoma she ever wanted to see. What had seemed like paradise in the letters now looked like a dusty, dirty little cotton town that had been stung by the oil bug. She'd drift through it for three hours and never look back.

The bitter north wind picked up speed and dust blew into her face. Few people were out and Addison didn't blame the rest for staying inside. She shoved her hands deeper into her coat pockets and wished for gloves but they were packed inside the trunk and she wasn't about to dig into her personal things right there in public.

"Cold, ain't it?" A lovely lady with dark hair and the clearest blue eyes Addison had ever seen sat down beside her on the bench. "You comin' or goin'?"

"Thought I was comin' until I got here. But now I guess I'm goin'," Addison said.

"I'm Tilly Sloan. Where you coming from? It's awfully cold to be sitting outside."

"I'm Addison Carter, coming from about as far east in Arkansas as you can go. With a good throwing arm, a body could pitch a rock across the Mississippi River into Tennessee. Thought I had a job but found out real quick some men can't abide a woman doctor."

Tilly nodded toward the door leading into the drug store. "You got that right. Want to come inside for a cup of hot chocolate or coffee?"

"I've got three hours before my ride takes me back to Ardmore. Something hot sounds good." Addison picked up her doctor's bag and carried it with her.

"That looks like . . ." Tilly opened the door.

"A doctor's bag? That's exactly what it is. Magnolia Oil hired me. I really am a doctor."

Tilly's eyes widened until they were as big and round as the moon. "Magnolia hired a woman?"

"No, they hired a man. They got a woman and fired her before she had time to sneeze. They hired me without an interview on the basis of my recommendations and good grades. I'm right out of medical school. Turned out they thought Addison was a man."

Tilly's laughter echoed through the whole drug store. "That's a hoot. So you're a doctor and they don't want you. Where are you going now?"

"They offered to buy me a ticket back to Arkansas, but I'm damn sure not going back."

"Get ya'll a cup of coffee?" Cornelia, the lady behind the fountain, asked.

"I'd like hot chocolate. Doc?" Tilly raised a dark eyebrow. She already liked the woman. Doctor or no, she had an attitude Tilly could relate to.

"I'll have the same and thanks for calling me Doc. I like that," Addison said.

"You are very welcome. Why aren't you going back?"

"Because my father and brother said I was wasting my time getting a medical degree. They said even though women can go to college now and get the training, I'd never find a job. When Magnolia hired me, I made them eat crow. I was a celebrity. There were going away parties. A huge story on the front page of the newspaper about women finally breaking into a man's field. Addison Carter was about to make her mark in the world. A woman doctor working for a big oil company in Oklahoma. If I went back, I'd be the laughing stock of the whole state."

Cornelia brought two steaming cups of hot chocolate. "How's Ford adjusting to the farm?" she asked Tilly.

"Right well. I swear he was born to be a farmer and just using the sheriff's badge to support himself until he found the right farm."

"Or the right woman," Cornelia smiled.

"I've only been married a couple of weeks. I fell in love with the sheriff and had to propose to him to get him to stay in town," Tilly explained.

"Congratulations. You proposed?" Addison sipped the chocolate. It did taste good. She hadn't eaten since early morning. She'd been too nervous for the lunch served on the train and too angry to eat after the men had dismissed her like something they'd tracked in on their boots.

"Woman's got to do what a woman's got to do. It was either propose and be happy, or let him go and be miserable. I don't like misery. Besides he's a natural born farmer. Just like I am."

"You don't look like a farmer. I'd have classified you as anything but a farmer. Maybe a model for one of those New York magazines."

"Keep talking, Doc, and I'll hire you myself."

Before Addison could reply the front door literally flew open and the north wind blew in another lady. She was as stunning as Tilly and her eyes were frantic.

"Tilly," she said breathlessly, "come quickly. Tucker's been hurt. Briar went over there and found him on the ground. He'd fallen off the barn roof. Looks like a leg's broken and who knows what else. We've got to go to Ardmore and bring a doctor. Ford and Briar have him up in his bedroom but he's not conscious and they're afraid to move him any more. He broke his pocket watch in the fall. Looks like he laid there for hours and he hasn't woke up yet."

"No we don't have to go to Ardmore. We've got a doctor right here. Come on Addison, I've got your first patient waiting. Hurry up. We'll help you load your things into my car and take you out to the Evening Star."

"But—" Addison started to protest.

"But nothing. You a doctor or not? Tucker may be dying. I need help and I don't have time to drive twenty-three miles to get one if you can fix him."

"I'll go but I might miss my ride," Addison thought out loud.

"I'll take you anywhere you want to go if you'll just

come with me and take care of Tucker." Tilly was already at the door and beginning to pick up luggage while she talked.

"Who's Tucker?" Addison asked as she helped Tilly load her big trunks into the automobile.

"He and the lady in the car ahead of me, Clara, are my cousins. But we were all born within months of each other and we're more like siblings. Tucker owns the farm right next to Clara's and not far from mine. And he's going to hate you, so get ready for it." Tilly drove like a bat set loose from the bowels of hell, cold dust boiling up behind her, knuckles white as she gripped the steering wheel, eyes scared half out of her mind.

"Why? What did I do?"

"You know how stubborn those men were at Magnolia Oil about having a woman doctor? Well, multiply that by ten and you've got Tucker Anderson."

"Hells bells." Addison's breath rushed out in a gush.

"Yep!" Tilly nodded and set her foot down even heavier on the gas pedal.

Tucker opened his eyes to find a witch not three inches from his face. Red hair cut right below her ears and kinking every which way around her face. Yellow flecks sprinkled in mossy green eyes, and a fair share of freckles dancing across her pert little nose.

"I hurt," he muttered.

"Of course you hurt. Be quiet and be still while I listen to your insides," she bossed.

So she didn't only look like something the cats drug in and the dogs wouldn't have for supper, she was sassy to boot. Tucker hated red-haired women. They always had a temper. He didn't like green eyes either. They reminded him of the black cat who clawed him when he was six years old. It had evil green eyes and he remembered yellow flecks in its eyes when it tried to take half the hide off his leg. He really, really didn't like sassy women. Not even if he was hurting so bad each breath felt like it was ripping his insides apart.

"Bruised muscles but I don't hear any gurgling in his lungs," she noted.

Tucker looked around the room. Clara and her husband, Briar. Tilly and her new husband, Ford. And the green-eyed monster with a stethoscope right on his bellybutton, which was entirely too personal for a nurse.

"I want a real doctor," he said loudly. Even if it did hurt to talk, he wasn't going to take some nurse's opinion as gospel.

"I am a real doctor and you're a real patient. A grouchy one but you're hurt. I've set your leg. You were spared that much as you slept. I stitched your hand where you landed on the shovel blade when you fell. It's a wonder you didn't break your fool neck or bleed to death." She finished listening to his heart and stomach and put the stethoscope back in her bag.

A fine heart beating soundly and the stomach behind those rigid muscles produced the right sounds. Tucker Anderson was a lucky man. With a fall like that he could have been crushed inside and on his death bed. Now the only thing he had to fear was dying of pure old cantankerousness.

"A woman doctor? Tilly?" Tucker glared at his cousin.

"Oh, hush. I'm giving you a shot of morphine so you can deal with the pain. You'll be out for a long time and when you wake up you'll be begging for more. Don't be fussing at your cousin. She's done you a big favor. I'm a damn good doctor even if I wear a dress and not pants." Addison shoved the needle into his arm.

"Get her out of here." He growled as the darkness of painless sleep overtook him.

"We probably need to take him to the hospital in Ardmore," Clara whispered.

"I wouldn't try to move him," Addison said. "He'd be better off right here with one of you coming to help him."

Tilly moaned. She'd only been married a short while. She sure didn't want to spend her days running back and forth to Tucker's bed to listen to him complain, grumble and grouse around all day long. She loved him like a brother but she'd be willing to give half a kingdom to get out of the job of taking care of him.

"Remember when we all had chicken pox?" she asked.

"And Tucker was worse than us girls," Clara nodded seriously.

"And measles, when he had to stay in a dark room for ten days. Remember?"

"Don't recall nightmares, Tilly." Clara sighed. She'd just found out she was pregnant. There was no way

Briar would consent to her running up and down stairs all day waiting on Tucker. She'd feel guilty if she didn't do her part, though, what with Tilly barely married two weeks.

"That bad, huh?" Addison asked.

"He's a good man, really. We love him like a brother, but he doesn't like being cooped up. He gets a little testy when he can't go outside," Tilly said.

"Well, he's probably going to be in this bed or on this floor for at least six weeks. Maybe by then with lots of help he'll be able to go outside," Addison said.

Ford eyed Addison closely. She'd done a professional job when she set that leg and her stitches were as fine as he'd ever seen. She was an excellent doctor, no doubt about it.

"What were you doing in Healdton?" he asked.

While she put her supplies away, she told him the short version of the trip, leaving out the part about being so mad and humiliated she could have committed homicide.

"So you in a hurry to go back to Arkansas?" He asked.

"Not on your life. I'm going to Ardmore to the hotel for tonight and tomorrow I'm talking to someone about enlisting as a nurse in the service. They'll take anyone and with my qualifications I should be sent to the front lines."

"Why not wait a few weeks? I'm sure Tilly and Clara would be glad to pay you a handsome salary to stay right here at the Evening Star ranch and take care of Tucker. Doctor's do private practice sometimes don't they?"

Tilly's eyes twinkled. "Oh, honey, name your price and I'll double the amount."

"The man hates me. He won't tolerate six weeks cooped up with someone he despises." Addison snapped the bag shut.

"So? We're not asking you to like him. Just take care of him. We'll even come around and do the outside chores. At least Ford and Briar will," Clara said.

Addison sat down in a rocking chair and thought about the proposition for a whole of two minutes. "I'll take the job. For six weeks. That's how long it will take his leg to heal. I'll go stark raving mad in a house with a man like him if I can't get out, so I'll do the chores. I'm accustomed to it. I grew up on a farm about like this one and I don't mind the work."

"Then the pay just tripled," Briar said. "I'll pay the last part and Ford and I will help out whenever you need us, anyway."

"You haven't even heard my price," Addison said.

"Whatever you say, you'll earn it. When he wakes up he's going to be worse than a hungry grizzly bear with an abscessed tooth and ingrown toenail. He's very independent and he doesn't think much of women doctors and lawyers," Clara said.

"Then my price is one hundred dollars a week," Addison said.

Good Lord, had she just named such an exorbitant

fee? Had she really said that out loud? They wouldn't want her to stay at that price. Perhaps in her subconscious she was trying to make it impossible for them to hire her.

"Done!" Tilly stuck out her hand to shake on the deal. "I'll give you twelve hundred and Briar is going to write you an extra six hundred when you leave for doing the chores."

"Are you serious?" Addison gasped.

"Oh, yes, ma'am," Ford grinned. "These girls never tease about money. But you'll earn it, Doc. Six weeks with this opinionated, cantankerous man and you'll be begging to go to the front lines. Tilly says he's just like his grandfather Anderson. I've had no trouble with Tucker. He and Briar, here, are my best friends. But you, being a lady Doc, you'll have a rough row to hoe. So if you want to back out, do it right now. When he wakes up, he's going to be a handfull."

"Oh, I think I can do the job. After all he's got a busted leg and he can't use his right hand. He can't chase me and he can't hit me. I expect I can give as good as he can when it comes to a verbal battle." Addison kept rocking.

Tilly grabbed Ford's hand and led him toward the door. "Then you've got a job. I'm going home. I'll be over tomorrow and check on you. And thanks, Doc."

Clara followed Tilly to the door. "You are an angel sent from heaven at the right moment. I'm sorry Magnolia treated you so badly, but I'm glad you didn't get out of town before we found you."

"Don't be too quick. You might be tossing me out on my ear in a few days. I'm not so easy to live with either so don't be calling me an angel. Tucker might insist you fire me."

Chapter Two

Addison was surprised to see both her trunks in the hallway. "Whew!" She exclaimed honestly, appreciating the two men who'd had the foresight to bring them up the stairs for her. They were very, very heavy and she'd have had to make many trips up and down if they hadn't taken care of it. There was no way she could have carried either of them without help. She eyed five doors: two opening off to the left, two to the right, and one at the end of the landing.

She peeked inside the room at the end. "Bathroom," she said with a nod. That would help tremendously. She wouldn't have to tote water to take care of her new patient and with a set of crutches he could take care of his own needs in a couple of days.

Choosing a room wasn't easy. They were all of a

size. All had a nice sized closet and lovely furniture, but each door she opened presented a messier room than the one before. Evidently Tucker never threw away a thing. Newspapers, especially, were stacked in every available space. She finally made her decision by bouncing on the mattresses. The room with the softest bed would be her bedroom for the next six weeks. It was right across the hallway from Tucker's room and the window looked out into the backyard.

She didn't have time to unpack or even drag her trunks into the room. It was time for chores and that was part of the job description. She opened the smallest chest and pulled out a pair of striped overalls and a faded flannel shirt. She had debated for an hour about using precious space to bring such things to her new prestigious job in Healdton, Oklahoma. Thank goodness common sense had won out over vanity. Once she'd changed, she checked the girl in the dingy cheval mirror. She looked more like a prepubescent boy than a doctor, but those pompous oil men hadn't even given her a chance to prove her worth.

She opened the door into Tucker's bedroom. He was breathing easily. The morphine had worked well. He'd be out for several more hours and that's what he needed—good, deep sleep until the initial shock of the fall wore off. After that, complete rest for a few weeks would be the prescription. He was lucky that it had been a clean break and didn't puncture the skin. She wished for one of those fancy new X-ray machines they'd shown the students in the last year of medical school. They'd been around for more than fifteen years but it was the first time she'd seen one. It would be years and years before she could afford such a thing in a private practice. She might as well wish for the moon.

Setting the leg hadn't been easy but she'd managed and using what she had in her medical trunk, she'd put a cast on it. Probably higher up on the leg than necessary but she wanted to make sure it was secure. She'd cleaned the hand and given him a tetanus shot. Thank goodness for the vaccine. Without it, the laceration on Tucker's hand could have become infected from the dirty shovel blade—a condition which could have led to death. Now at least he had a fighting chance to live and, hopefully, recover total use of his right hand and his leg.

She wasn't sure where to begin since no one had shown her the exact locations of the animals, but she heard a cow bawling off to the south and figured she'd start there. The keys were in the pickup truck so she backed it into the hay barn not far from the house, found a set of hooks and loaded enough for a good sized herd. She drove south and found the herd lined up behind a barbed wire fence waiting. Not so different than what she'd seen in Arkansas the week before. Only this week she was supposed to have left all that behind.

The wind had not died down a bit and wheezed through the bare tree branches like an old man with bronchitis singing with in the church choir. She crawled up in the back of the truck and cut the twine holding the hay bale together, then picked it up carefully and tossed it over the fence. She didn't know how well Tucker fed his cattle but she wasn't letting anything in her jurisdiction go hungry and there appeared to be lots of hay in the barn. The cattle were well fed that evening.

Little more than an hour later the livestock, including chickens and a half dozen hogs, were fed. She was glad she hadn't found a cow to milk. Even though she could do the job, it was one she really didn't like. She'd always passed it off to her brother, Luke, whenever possible. Dusk settled around her like a cold shroud as she parked the truck and started across the yard. A big yellow dog came out to greet her from the porch. She stopped in her tracks, wondering how she'd get in the house if the dog wasn't friendly, but he wagged his tail, dropped his head and begged to be petted.

She scratched his ears. "What's your name fellow? Are you hungry too? Been taking care of the place all day? I'll find food for you, I promise. You won't go hungry. Where do you sleep? You keep watch and I'll go see what I can rustle up."

Groping around with one hand in the air and her eyes peeled toward the ceiling, she finally found the cord and brought light into the kitchen. Considering what she'd found in the bedrooms, it was amazingly tidy. One plate, cup and saucer attested to the fact that Tucker had eaten sometime that day before he took the nose dive off the barn roof. She quickly inventoried the pantry and found enough food to last a month or more. But what took her eye was the Kelvinator refrigerator. She'd read that there were about two dozen home refrigerators introduced to the U.S. market the previous year and right there in front of her was the very one she'd seen in the magazine. While she looked at the contraption in awe, a strange noise let her know the compressor had kicked on. It had to be located in the basement and driven by belts attached to motors located there just like the article said. The whole thing fascinated her. She opened the door and cold air rushed out. Inside she found cold milk, half a ham, butter, eggs.

"Holy Mother of God, these people are rich. If they can afford something like this, they'd sneeze at the paltry amount I demanded." She took out bacon and eggs to make a simple supper.

When she turned around she was facing a Souvenir Cast Stove: sparkling, shiny clean and new. Blue, so bright it glowed like a midnight sky. Two tiles in the back decorated with pink roses. Gleaming metal legs and the fire box was already laid full and waiting for the match. Cooking in this kitchen was going to be so much fun she might never want to leave. She'd already cut strips of bacon and had it sizzling in a cast iron skillet when she remembered the dog. She didn't have any idea what Tucker usually fed him but tonight he was having a half dozen scrambled eggs. She placed them in a bowl and carried them to the cabinet. In a separate skillet she melted butter and fixed the eggs as perfectly as if they were for the governor of Arkansas. The dog waited on the back porch and wagged his tail fast and furious in thanks.

It was evident that Tucker lived alone and there hadn't been a woman present in a very long time. The dining room, living room, his office and the foyer were all piled high with newspapers just like the bedrooms. She wondered if he collected the things. She picked one from the stack nearest to the table and read as she ate two strips of bacon, a slab of bread and two fried eggs. The banner said it was *The Daily Ardmoreite*. According to the front page news from six months ago, Dr. James Smith was on the sick list. The doctor had been answering calls day and night and refusing to take the rest he so badly needed, and at last had to go to bed himself. The reporter said it was not the influenza, but Dr. Smith would be forced to take a rest so that he would be able to leave for camp within the next fifteen days to assume his duties as a captain in the medical corps.

"Hmmm," she mumbled as she ate. She'd seen similar articles in her local newspaper. Doctors everywhere were leaving to offer their services to the war effort. She noticed an article about a man who had been reared in Ardmore but now resided in Norman. He had just come home from the war. His wife, who was also a doctor, had kept up his practice—as well as her home and their two children—while he was away. Now that he was home, she would turn the practice over to him.

"How nice! She can stay home and be a sweet little homemaker. God, save me from riding into the profession on the coattails of a husband. I'll make it on my own or quit all together," Addison muttered but kept scanning for anything about Healdton.

"Marble flooring for the remodeled bank has been received and will be laid as soon as the workmen can get to it. All the copper for the marquees has arrived and it will be placed as soon as that part of the work can be gotten to. The remodeling job is going to make a beauty in every particular and will be in keeping with the splendid advancement the institution is making under the capable and popular management of President Clifford Williams and Cashier Ralph Dixon. Teller Olivia Traversty said she thought the marble flooring was going to be 'just lovely,' and she is glad to be working at the bank." Addison read aloud to an empty room.

She filled her mouth with the last of the toast and found out there had been a robbery at the Drug Store on Main Street in Healdton. Items amounting to between fifty and one hundred dollars were stolen during the night. Entrance was gained through a window in the rear of the basement, and departure taken through the side door of the basement which was found open the next morning. The burglar helped himself to a case of aspirin, two bottles of cough syrup and other sundry items. Officers were working on the case, but it was reported they had no tangible clue early the morning of the publication. Inez Simpson was the wife of the owner, George Simpson. She operated the soda counter and was quoted to say that she was terrified and hoped they found the culprit soon but one never knew who the robber might be with so many new faces brought into town with the oil boom.

"Thank goodness I wasn't in town or they'd have blamed me for the robbery. New doctor. Can't afford to buy medicine so I steal it. What kind of place have I come to?" She tossed the paper aside and cleaned up after herself in the kitchen.

She remembered the light cord hanging down the staircase had a wooden thread spool on the end. She crossed the cluttered dining room and foyer to pull it before she turned out the kitchen light. Maneuvering her way through the obstacle course was difficult enough with light. Doing so in the dark would put her in bed with a worse broken leg than Tucker's. Her goal that evening was to make the room she'd call hers the next six weeks livable. She wasn't a bit sleepy and the morphine she'd given Tucker would surely keep him resting until midnight so she had lots of time.

The first order of business was to tote all the unnecessary papers from her room to any one of the other three. When Tucker awoke she'd ask him what he intended to do with the massive collection. She picked up an armload and carried them across the hall and went back for more when she heard a moan from his room.

She peeked inside to see him staring blankly at the ceiling. She brushed her hands on the seat of her overalls and stepped inside the room. She'd shed her work shoes at the back door so she padded barefoot across the cold hardwood floor to his bedside.

"Who in the hell are you?" Steely blue eyes glared at her.

"I'm Dr. Addison Carter. Your cousins, Clara and Tilly, have hired me to take care of you for the next six weeks. I've set your leg, stitched your hand, and given you a tetanus vaccination and a dose of morphine. I'm surprised you are awake so soon. Figured you'd sleep until midnight or later." She picked up her stethoscope and threw back the quilt.

"What are you doing?" He asked thickly, trying to swim up from a drug induced sleep that kept pulling him back under.

"I'm listening to your heart and stomach. I want to be sure there's no internal damage." She unfastened two buttons on his long handles and set the cold metal on his stomach.

He pointed toward the door with his left hand. "Get out of here. I don't need you."

"You've got to have help and I took the job. Now hush so I can hear."

"You're not a doctor. Women aren't doctors."

"Oh, but I am, and I'm here for six weeks whether you like it or not, Mr. Anderson. Your heart still sounds good and your internal organs are making the right noises. I think I'd be safe in saying everything inside is fine. Just lots of bruises, a busted leg and a cut on your right hand."

He held his bandaged hand up and tried desperately to focus on it. There appeared to be one and a half hands in front of his eyes. "It hurts," he said.

"Sure it does. I put six stitches across your palm. The shovel you fell on was made of steel, not scrambled eggs. Are you hungry?"

"No. My stomach doesn't feel so good."

"Effects of the morphine. It does that to some people. We'd best not give you any more." She shook a thermometer while she talked.

"I don't have fever," he grumbled. "And you are not staying so don't get comfortable."

"We'll see." She shoved the thermometer toward him.

Instinctively, he opened his mouth and concentrated on holding the glass tube under his tongue. He remembered being on the roof and kicking his hammer out of reach without meaning to. When he reached for it, he lost his balance. He awoke in his bed with his entire body hurting. He vaguely remembered Tilly and Clara being in the room. What in the devil had they done?

"I'm getting up," he said around the thermometer.

"Not tonight you aren't. We'll talk about it in a couple of days. Maybe then with crutches and only to the bathroom and back. Right now, you're in bed until I say so."

"I'll do what I damn well please." He hoped he sounded as disgusted as he felt.

"Shhh!" She shushed and checked the thermometer. "No fever. That's a good sign. I was worried about that hand. I cleaned it as well as I could, but you never know about all the germs on a garden tool."

"Woman, I'm getting up!"

"I'm the doctor and I said no."

"I don't care if you are God. I've got to go to the bathroom or else these sheets are going to be wet," he blushed scarlet.

"Well, why didn't you say so instead of getting all huffy about everything." She disappeared out the door and returned quickly with a quart jar. "This can be your urinal for the next couple of days. I have a bedpan in my medical trunk if you need it for . . ."

"Give me that and get out," he growled.

"Just sit it on the bedside table and I'll take care of it when you are finished. Mr. Anderson, I am a doctor. Bodily functions are natural."

"Go!"

"Lord, save me from a prissy old bachelor," she muttered as she shut the door behind her. She gave him a full five minutes before she went back inside to find the jar sitting on the table and his eyes shut.

She held the jar up to the hallway light. "Good color. If the kidney was damaged there would be blood by now."

Tucker's eyes snapped open. "Have you no shame?"

"Not where my profession is concerned. I thought you'd be glad to hear some good news." She carried the jar to the bathroom and disposed of its contents, washed it out and brought it back. "It'll be right here if you need it in the night. And by the way, I'm setting up shop in the room right across the hall. What do you want me to do with your collection of newspapers?"

He moaned.

"I guess I'd moan too, if I'd been too lazy to dispose of papers for a hundred years."

"I hurt and you want me to talk about newspapers," he grumbled.

"Well, you can't have any more morphine until after midnight."

"Open that drawer and get me a BC Powder." He nodded toward the bedside table.

"Oh, so you need me to do something, do you?"

"What are they paying you?"

"Why?"

"I'll double it if you leave," he said.

"No thank you. I agreed on a price for a job and I'll do it. Now let me help you sit a little if you want a BC Powder. It might help you relax and it sure couldn't hurt."

"Don't need your help." Everything in the room took a spin when he used his left arm and tried to drag himself into a sitting position. He broke out in a weak sweat and his stomach did at least three flops before it settled down.

She stood beside the bed with her arms crossed over her chest. The arrogant, opinionated jackass could get his own BC Powder and swallow it with what saliva he could produce or choke to death on it.

He looked up at her with cold blue eyes. "You're getting paid to help me so do it."

"Please?"

"I've died and gone to hell," he mumbled. "Please!"

"Thank you." She found the medication, shook a folded glassine paper from the red, white and blue container, and unwrapped it. "Want it on your tongue or mixed with water?" She carefully poured a tumbler full from the pitcher on his table. Old women usually demanded water on their tables. Handsome men didn't. She was right. He was a prissy bachelor.

"On my tongue." He opened his mouth.

She slowly administered the white powder and handed him the water. "So you've died and gone to hell? So have I, Tucker Anderson. Now what do you want me to do with all those newspapers?"

"Burn 'em," he said after he'd finished half the water.

"Why haven't you?"

"None of your business," he said. "I'm going back to sleep."

"That's the best news I've had all day," she said.

Chapter Three

Smoke rose in spiraling circles from the burning barrel in the back yard. Addison had filled it to the brim with newspapers, some dated back ten years, before she lit it. Wind whipped her skirt tail around her ankles and crept up her legs. She shivered in spite of the heavy coat she'd found on the hook beside the back door. There'd be hoboes down in their shanty huts who'd probably love to warm their hands by the heat produced that bitter cold morning. Or maybe folks who still lived in tents out in Wirt, those waiting for an oil company house to be built or become available. Too bad she couldn't pipe the warmth to those in need.

"Hello," a voice called from the porch.

Addison whipped around to see a young woman waving. It wasn't Tilly or Clara. She'd recognize their

27

dark hair from a hundred feet away and through a smoke fog.

"We came to help," the lady called.

Addison left her fire. Help, in any form, wouldn't be turned away and would surely be appreciated. "I'm Dr. Addison Carter." She extended her hand when she reached the back porch.

"I'm Olivia. My husband is Julius Avery. He's a preacher. He's up there with Tucker right now. I brought a pot of beans and a pan of cornbread. Tilly said they'd hired you to take care of him. Julius has visits to make today so I thought I'd stay and help you." Olivia shook her hand firmly.

"Thank you," Addison said. "I've already got the morning chores done and dealt with the old bear up there. I could use some help burning all these blasted newspapers."

"Old bear?" Olivia's brown eyes twinkled. "Time was when I thought he was the most handsome thing in this part of the state. Even fancied that I might get him to marry me."

"Why didn't he?" Addison liked Olivia instantly. Her face was honest and open; her eyes were full of life.

"Because he outran me. Julius didn't." She looped her arm through Addison's.

"Look who I found out back burning papers," Olivia said when they reached Tucker's room. "Julius, this is Dr. Addison Carter. Dr. Carter, my husband, Julius."

"I'm glad to meet you." Addison shook his hand and glanced over at Tucker.

"You're burning what?" He asked.

"Newspapers and magazines. This place is a fire hazard," she said.

"Who gave you permission to burn my property?" He glared.

"You did. Last night when you were being as cranky as you are right now I asked what you wanted me to do with all those papers and you said to 'burn 'em'."

Tucker searched in the foggy memories he'd had since the accident and somewhere he did remember telling her to burn the papers. Actually, he'd been planning to get rid of them for a very long time. The last years of his father's life, he'd gotten into the habit of stacking his papers beside the chair in the living room when he finished reading them. When the pile reached the top of the arm of the chair, he'd tote them into one of the unused bedrooms. Two men and no women lived in the house on Evening Star ranch. They hardly ever had company—other than Tilly who didn't keep house any better, and Clara, who seldom left Healdton—so it didn't matter if there were papers everywhere. There was no sentimental value to them but he'd never let her know that. He didn't want her there. He didn't believe in women doing what was and would always be men's professions. Society had opened a big box of worms when they let women go to medical school. Before long, they'd have the right to vote and after that they'd want to run for mayor and governor, maybe even president.

Addison ignored the angry looks her patient shot her way and studied the preacher. A small nondescript man who didn't match Olivia for beauty or personality. But the way he looked at his wife was exactly what Addison wanted if she ever found a husband. Pure, unadulterated adoration. Olivia looked at him the same way. The bloom was certainly still on the marriage.

"Well, it looks like you are in the best of hands, Tucker. I can't imagine how Tilly and Clara talked a real doctor into staying with you, but you must be the luckiest man on earth. Tilly tells me she's doing the chores and if she's burning papers, she must be cleaning out this boar's nest, too. The angels surely favored you when they put Tilly in contact with Dr. Carter. You must be doing something right for God to rain such blessings down on you," Julius said.

Tucker barely grunted. Blessings! A weed might be called a flower in some folk's thinking, but it didn't change the fact it was a weed. Dr. Addison Carter was not a blessing of any kind. Rained down? Most likely shot upward with smoke still hanging on her skirt tails.

"I'll be gone most of the day but I'll be back before supper," Julius said to Olivia.

"Why don't I just make something here? That way Dr. Carter won't have to cook today." Olivia looked at Addison for approval.

"That would be wonderful, and please call me Addy.

My friends all just call me Addy. I'd like it if both of you would.

"Okay, then Addy, it is," Julius smiled.

Olivia wrapped her arms around Julius' neck. "Kiss me, darlin', and we'll see you this afternoon." She leaned forward and Julius had no choice but to kiss her.

Addison blushed and looked away from the newly wedded couple to find Tucker with so much crimson in his cheeks that for a moment she was afraid he'd spiked a fever.

"I'm aching everywhere." Tucker leaned back on the pillows.

"I'm sure you are and you will be for several days. You're fortunate that you are alive and didn't break your neck," Addison said. "I could give you another dose of morphine or some BC Powder."

"Just the powders. I don't like the feeling that morphine gives me."

"Which room are you working on first?" Olivia asked. "I'll get busy keeping that fire fed. Too bad we can't put that heat in a container and use it in the house."

"Right across the hall." Addison carefully poured the medicine on Tucker's tongue and gave him a glass of water. He didn't handle it very well with his left hand and spilled a little on his chin. She wiped it away instantly with a cloth she kept on the bedside table.

"Where?" His deep blue eyes widened.

"Across the hall."

Olivia passed the doorway carrying so many newspapers she could hardly see over the top of the stack.

"You cannot stay in that room," he declared.

"Why not? All the rooms are the same size and that one has the softest mattress."

"It's my parents' room and besides as soon as Tilly gets here today, I'm firing you. Clara and Tilly are both playing a joke on me because I don't like women doctors. They can find a man to do the chores and a lady to cook for me. You'll be gone by supper. Maybe Julius can take you back into town."

"Quit being such a baby. I'll be right here for six weeks. That was the deal and your cousins aren't going to break their word."

"We'll see." He shut his eyes and ignored the lady. He wasn't going to refer to her as a doctor, not even in his mind. She was a red-haired witch and he'd always despised redheads. They were always hot-tempered and the almighty Addison—or was it Addy, she said her friends called her?—had just proven his point. Everything he said, she had an argument. He'd fallen and broken his leg, but that wasn't the end of the world. With a set of crutches he could manage very well. He fell asleep planning a stinging speech for his two cousins.

Addison met Olivia in the foyer, coming back for more papers. "Hey, I just got an idea on the way down. What if we opened the bedroom window over on that side of the house, tied them up in bundles and threw them out. I'll keep the fire going if you'll bundle and toss."

"I'll keep the fire going. That way if Tucker needs help, you'll be right there. That's a wonderful plan. Leave it to a couple of women to get things done right," Olivia said.

"Amen, sister."

"I'll go with you and help bundle a few while the ones that I already stuffed in the barrel are burning." Olivia followed Addison.

"You and Julius haven't been married long?" Addison retrieved a spool of cord from the kitchen she'd seen that morning.

"About two months," Olivia said. "I was Olivia Traversty before. Worked at the bank as a teller."

"I read your name in an old paper last night. Something about the bank getting a new floor." Addison led the way into the bedroom across from Tucker.

"Oh, yes, my one claim to fame. That and the day I was hauled out of there after a robbery and held hostage for several hours. Tilly came and saved me." Olivia made a neat stack and tied it down.

"Now that's a story. Tell me," Addison said.

"Well, Red Johnson got liquored up and robbed the bank. Grabbed me by the hair and threw me up on his horse and took me out to his house. He held off the deputy for several hours and then Ford came. He was the sheriff then and trying his dead level best to prove

Carolyn Brown

Tilly was a moonshine runner. Anyway, Tilly just came barging in that house like a bolt of thunder. She talked Red into letting me go, then took his shotgun away from him and brought him out the door. He's still in jail for the robbery. Until next fall sometime. Hand me the string. I've got two bundles ready. By the way, you have the prettiest red hair I've ever seen."

"Thank you. I've always hated it. That's why when some women started wearing short hair, I had it cut. My brother says it looks an old mop that's been hung out on the clothesline to dry."

"That's what makes it so pretty. My hair is straight as a board. I'd just love to have the nerve to cut it off right under my ears. But Julius loves it and I wouldn't upset him for anything. I think that's got enough to keep the fires going a while. You know we might get the upstairs at least mucked out today with this plan."

"Did Tilly really run moonshine?" Addison asked.

"Can't prove it. No one could but maybe Bessie and Beulah. They were friends of her grandmother's. Miss Katy Evening Star Hawk Anderson. Indian woman who married Tucker's grandfather and ran shine right under his nose for a long time before she ever told him. Bessie and Beulah were her cohorts. They bought the Morning Glory Inn when Clara married Briar. Now that's another story. Anyway, Bessie is dead so if she knew Tilly was running shine, she took the truth to the grave with her. Beulah is up in years but still spry. I expect she'd go to hell and face the devil before she'd admit that Tilly ran shine and get her into trouble."

"Good friends like that are worth more than dollars," Addison said.

"You got that right. Start throwing Doc, and I'll shove it in the barrel. See you at lunch. By then we'll both be hungry as bear cubs."

"I know I will be. Bet my patient will be too." Addison carried two bundles to the window, opened it and tossed them out. Cold wind rushed inside the room, blowing the dingy lace curtains back in her face. Washing them would be a job for another day. Like Olivia said, mucking out was the first order of business. After that, she'd worry about cleaning.

At noon, all three bedrooms were free of papers. Addison and Olivia sighed when they met in the kitchen. Plain red beans with ham hock and cornbread had never smelled so good.

"How much did we get done?" Olivia asked.

"All the bedrooms are cleared out. You've got a smudge of soot on your ear." Addison handed her a wet cloth from the edge of the sink.

"Got it?" Olivia rubbed the cloth over her ear and the side of her face.

"Yes, it's all gone. How did you stay so clean out there among that burning mess?"

"Toss them in and then sit on the porch until that bunch is ashes. My job was really pretty easy and all that fire kept the area toasty warm. Did Tucker ever wake up?" Olivia asked.

"Not yet, but he's going to if I have to holler at him. A man has to eat good if he's to get his strength back. He swears he's going to fire me as soon as Tilly and Clara come to see him today. He really does hate women doctors doesn't he?" Addison prepared a tray with a bowl of beans, cornbread, a thick slice of red onion and a couple of dill pickles. She added a tall glass of cold milk and a napkin.

"Says he does. He can get on a soapbox about women doing a man's work real quick. But don't you worry none about losing your job. Clara and Tilly won't fire you and besides they're meaner than he thinks he is. You take that on up to him and I'll bring ours. We can eat with him. Food goes down better with good company. About his attitude: Maybe you'll change his mind like Briar did Clara's."

"You've got to tell me that story," Addison said.

"I'd be glad to. While we eat." Olivia began dipping up their lunch and setting it on a separate tray.

The aroma of ham and beans floating up to his bedroom awoke Tucker. His stomach growled. At least he'd have one good meal before he got rid of the woman. Before he could get his eyes fully open, she was there, dinner in her hands.

"Time to wake up and eat, Mr. Anderson." She didn't put the food in front of him but set in on the floor beside the bed. "I'll help you sit up and get you a wet cloth for your face and hands. Oh, dear, we must shave you this afternoon. I should have done that already this morning. You really have a heavy beard."

"No woman has ever shaved me and you ain't starting now," he grumbled.

She slipped an arm around his shoulders and brought him to a sitting position. She propped several pillows behind him and disappeared long enough to wring out a wash cloth. When she returned she washed his face without even asking him if he could do it himself.

Her fingertips were soft and gentle, reminding him of his mother washing his face when he was a little boy. But there was something else. A tingling way down deep in his gut like nothing he'd experienced before.

"You think you can manage to eat with your left hand?" She asked.

"Before I'd let you feed me, I could eat with my toes."

"Good. That's the spirit!" She'd tied the napkin around his neck like a bandana and draped it down over his chest.

Olivia brought their lunch inside the room and gave him her brightest smile. "We thought we'd eat with you. A bedroom picnic so you wouldn't have to eat alone."

"Whatever you want." His hand shook as he crumbled cornbread into the bowl of beans.

Addison and Olivia sat on the floor beside the bed. "Now tell me the story of Clara and Briar. You said she used to own some Morning Flower Hotel?" Addison said.

"The Morning Glory Inn. A boarding house. Anyway, she hated oil men. Said they'd torn up her way of life as much as the Civil War had the southern states. She was a bit odd in those days. Begging your pardon, Tucker, but she was. She went into town at three o'clock every single day for a whole year after she'd been jilted ten years before. Folks said she'd sit on the bench outside the Drug Store for an hour. Didn't matter if it was raining, snowing or in the middle of a twister. Some preacher came to Healdton for a revival and stayed at her boarding house. Proposed and said he'd come back and get her in a week. They'd elope and he'd take her to Louisiana where he had this big mansion and a church and everything. So she went every day to wait for him. I thought it was crazy but I soon learned it wasn't to welcome him into her arms but to take out revenge on the sorry fool." Olivia stopped to eat a few bites. "Anyway by the time I was living at the Morning Glory she wasn't going to town to sit on the bench but she did go every day at the exact same time to get the mail. Folks could set their clocks by her."

"So what happened?" Addison loved a good story.

"She was in town and while she was out, Dulcie, that was her cook, rented the room to Briar Nelson who was and is an oil man. Owns Rose Oil Company. Anyway she found out he was an oil man at a poetry reading and you'd have thought the world had come to an end. She trotted herself over to the sheriff and demanded he tell Briar to get out of the Morning Glory. Sheriff said he couldn't since Briar had signed a lease and unless he broke the terms of the lease, then Clara had to hold up her end of the bargain. We all figured it would be the very thing that sent her off to the asylum. But it just stiffened up her backbone. She quit going to town and she concentrated on fighting with that man. Took all summer but they fell in love and got married."

"Wow," Addison said. "That's a 'happily ever after' story."

"It was because of Libby," Tucker said from the bed. He'd never let them know it but listening to their conversation was entertaining and made him forget his aches and pains.

"Oh, pshaw!" Olivia blew out at him. "She adores that child but she's so in love with Briar it's amazing. He brought her out of that self-induced pity and made her see the person she was meant to be. Just like Julius did me."

"Oh?" Addison raised an eyebrow and hoped for another story.

"Fooled us all. Flighty as a hare in spring time and settling down with the preacher," Tucker said.

"Yes, I was. I'll admit it. I was running from myself. I woke up and realized I wasn't happy with the new person I'd created about the time Julius stepped into my life. I love him as much as Clara does Briar. You married? Your husband off in the war?" She looked at Addison.

"No, not married. Never have been. I hired on with

Magnolia Oil to take care of their employees and also the citizens in the area. Turned out they thought they were hiring a man since my name is Addison. I had the job about ten seconds after I got into Healdton and they found out I was a woman," she said.

"They might be the smartest men on the earth. They fired you, did they? I'm going to do the same thing," Tucker declared.

Olivia shook her spoon at him. "Tucker, you pompous jackass. And that's not an ugly word. It's in the Bible and you're being one. This woman is a god-send and you're saying mean things like that? What is the matter with you? I'm glad I didn't marry you."

"I never asked you." He finished off his milk without getting a drop on his napkin. He'd show them all he could run a farm with a busted hand and a broken leg. He was an Anderson. He could do anything.

"No, you didn't, but it's only because I didn't really set my heart on you. Old and slow as you are I could have caught you in a race. You're being mean and hateful to Addy, and I won't have it."

"She's going to be gone by dusk," Tucker declared.

"Oh?" Tilly said from the doorway.

"I don't think so." Clara chimed in right behind her.

"You two don't run the Evening Star. I do, and I'm not having a woman doctor taking care of me or this ranch. Bring me some crutches and I'll show you that I don't need any of you," he said.

"Beans sure smell good. Got any left in the kitchen?" Tilly asked.

Tucker pointed at her. "Don't you dare leave in the middle of a fight." He was getting really quick at using that left handed forefinger. By the time his hand healed, he might be able to use the left one as well as the right.

Tilly took two steps forward and leaned right down into his face. "Ain't no fight here, Tucker. We hired Doc. She's staying. You want crutches? You take that up with her. She's the boss for the next six weeks. We want you healed proper, not limping around like Curtis Weatherly. That man doctor who set his leg didn't make him stay off it for the right time and he'll never be whole again. Looks to me like she's already earned half her wages in just one day. So hush your mouth and take your medicine. Six weeks and then you can have the Evening Star back. Until then . . ."

"Clara, talk sense to her," he butted in.

"Why? She's the one talking sense. You're the pig-headed one here, Tucker. We're very glad to have a doctor willing to stop what she was doing and take care of you. Grow up," Clara said.

Tucker didn't want to limp for the rest of his life. He wanted to run the Evening Star until he was an old, old man. He wanted to sit on the porch and watch his great-grandchildren chase lightning bugs in the evening, but admitting he needed a doctor, a woman one at that, to ever realize his dreams, was as hard as eating live toad frogs.

"I'll be living in hell for six weeks with her," he moaned.

"Oh, my feelings are hurt." Addison wiped away fake tears. "When I first looked at you, all broken and bloody, the clouds parted and I thought I'd died and gone straight to heaven."

All four women burst into giggles.

Tucker couldn't figure out what was so funny.

Chapter Four

It was nothing short of a Mexican standoff. The room was toasty warm with extra wood in the heater but the water grew cold in the blue granite wash pan. Addison stood, wash cloth in hand beside the bed. Tucker had the sheet pulled up to his neck in a death grip. Neither was about to lose an inch of pride.

"You are not giving me a bath," he gritted his teeth.

"I am a doctor and I'm giving you a bath, but my patience is wearing thin, Tucker Anderson. You've been in that bed two nights now and you need cleaning up." Addison tugged at the sheet but he was stronger. "You give me one good reason why you won't let me give you a bed bath."

"You are a woman, that's why." He raised his voice.

"It's all right for a male doctor to see a woman so

43

what's wrong with me seeing you? If you'll all that modest, I'll wash you down to the waist and up to the knees and you can take care of the rest."

"That's not even decent," he protested.

"Water's getting colder by the minute and I'm not going to heat it up. Either drop the sheet and let me help you shave, bathe and wash that dirty hair, or I'll get a pair of scissors and cut it away from your hands."

"You wouldn't dare!" He glared at her.

"Oh, honey, I've dealt with professional cranky old men. You're just an amateur. When we finish cleaning you up, you're going to sit in that rocking chair while I change your sheets. So get ready for your first trip across the room." She tried a little psychology, hoping that the idea of getting out of bed would appeal to him.

"I can do most of it after you shave me?" He eyed her. "No tricks."

"No tricks," she agreed.

"I don't trust you," he declared.

"Feeling's mutual. Let go of the sheet and we'll get you in a sitting position then start to work."

He relaxed his grip and shut his eyes. He might have to endure such an abomination but he didn't have to like it.

She tossed half a dozen pillows on the floor and set him up straight in the bed. She lathered up the wash cloth and started with his hair; black as midnight, thick long. She worked the soap down to his scalp with her fingertips and massaged.

He bit back a moan. It was pure luxury to have someone wash his hair. Every nerve in his body tingled. Using the cloth, she continued the job until there were no suds left, and then brushed it all back away from his face. Before he could protest, she had the soap cup in her hand and his face covered in thick lather.

He tensed at the thought of a woman using a straight razor so close to his jugular vein, but in a moment he relaxed. Her fingers were light on his skin as she removed two days worth of heavy beard in deft swipes. She splashed Witch Hazel on his face when she finished and patted it dry with a towel.

"I'm going to wash your back. First I'm going to unbutton your long handles just across your chest. You reckon you could wash your front side?" She'd learned men didn't think their back was as intimate as their fronts. She could feel the muscles tense before she ever started but it only took a moment until he was putty in her hands.

"I can do it when you finish with my back," he said but the anger was gone from his voice.

"Well, we'll have to get your long handles off. You have any pajamas in the house?"

"I can take them off by myself. Get me some scissors to cut the bottom half away from the cast. Pajamas are in my top drawer." He motioned toward the oak chest of drawers across the room. If she thought she was going to peel his underwear off him, she was certifiably goofy.

She finished his back and found the pale blue cotton pajamas. She laid them on the rocking chair, the promise of getting out of bed tempting him.

"Now I'm going to change the dressing on your hand and check the wound. We'll take the stitches out in two weeks. That's twelve more days and then I'll begin some therapy so you won't lose the use of your fingers." She talked as she cut away the bandage and cleaned the wound. The stitches looked clean. No infection or red lines shooting out from the cut. That alone was a miracle but she wouldn't mention it to him as skittish as he was. She washed his hand well, taking time to clean under his nails and trim them with her small suture scissors.

"Now I'm going to leave and let you finish your bath. I don't know how you'll get those long handles completely off without help but if you think you can do it, have at it. When you finish call me. You can hold the sheet up to protect your modesty and I'll help you put your pajamas on.

"Just get out."

"Yes, sir."

She sat outside the door on a chair and listened to his moans and groans but he didn't call out for her to help. In twenty minutes a weak voice said he was ready.

Picking up the shirt to the pajamas she held it out and he let go of one side of the sheet and put his one arm into a sleeve. She moved around the bed and he repeated the process. She buttoned it for him and waited for him to pull the sheet up to his knees, revealing a leg in a cast and one freshly washed one.

He groaned when she took a pair of scissors and cut more than half the leg from his pajama bottoms.

"Hush," she said.

"They're ruined now."

"So are the long johns you cut off." She pointed at the floor where they lay in a heap.

"I hate wasting a good pair of long johns or pajamas," he said.

"They were ruined already. I cut the whole left leg out of them when I set your leg so stop moaning and groaning. It won't cause the bank to foreclose on your ranch if you have to buy another pair." She slipped the short leg over the cast and tugged them up to his knee.

"That hurts," he said.

"Hey, is this the man who can run a ranch with a cast on one leg and a bandage on his right hand?" She finished the job, shut the door behind her and waited in the hall again.

Tucker sweated bullets trying to raise his hips without sending shock waves of pure pain down his legs. By the time he finished getting them where they belonged, he was literally trembling with exhaustion but he managed.

She knocked on the door but didn't wait for an answer before plowing right in, not at all surprised to see him clean and clothed, the top sheet thrown off on the floor. "Good job, Mr. Anderson, but you're as pale as a set of bleached bones. If you're not able to get to the rocking chair with my help, I do know how to remake a bed with you in it."

"I can sit up in a chair. It's layin' up here in this bed that's making me weak. If you'd have let me get up yesterday I'd be stronger. A man wasn't meant to wallow around in bed after the sun is up."

"Okay then, let's get that strength built back. Here're your crutches. I had Tilly buy them when she was in Ardmore yesterday. First I'll help you swing the cast off the side of the bed and then I want you to sit for a few minutes with your legs dangling."

"Legs don't dangle. I'm tall enough my feet hit the ground," he said.

And they did. She'd realized he was a tall man. Well built. Muscular from his farm work, but he was taller than she'd expected. She sat in the rocking chair and stared at him. Color drained from his face. A fine bead of sweat popped up under his nose. She gave his nervous system five minutes to get out of the habit of lying prone.

She held the crutches out to him. "Time to see if you can use these things. Go slow and easy at first. If you need to sit down, sink back, don't fall. Easy now." She supported him under one arm while he made a feeble attempt to stand.

He ground his jaw teeth to keep from admitting that his leg throbbed and his hand threatened to break off if he didn't stop putting pressure on his fingers with the crutch. Nothing in his thirty years had prepared him for a broken leg on one side of his body and an extremely sore hand on the other. He was more than glad someone was there with him, even a red-haired witch woman doctor, to help him maneuver from the bed to the chair. He'd walked less than five feet and he felt as if he'd just walked the fence line all the way around the ranch.

She placed the crutches on the floor beside the chair and went straight to the task of remaking the bed. Dirty linens were tossed out into the hallway to be washed on Monday. When she finished the bed was hospital regulation tight. That done, she went to work on the room. One stack of newspapers had already been burned but the stack in the corner beside his chair was at least two feet tall. She shot it an evil look, determined to take care of it tomorrow when he was sleeping. In half an hour, the bedside table was straight, the floor swept clean and mopped, the furniture dusted.

"Had enough sitting up?" She asked.

"No, I'm going to the bathroom." He reached for the crutches.

"It'll wear you out. I told you I have a bedpan."

"I'm going to the bathroom." He left no room for argument. "Help me."

She raised an eyebrow.

"I gave you an order. You are paid help and you'll follow orders." The minute the words were out of his mouth he wished he could take them back. He'd never been so cross with anyone in his life. He was a fair man with his hired help and not once had he been such an old crank pot. But damn it all, Tilly and Clara had no right to hire a woman doctor when they knew exactly how he felt about them. It was their fault.

She raised the other eyebrow.

"You are fired."

"Okay. I'll pack my things and leave. I don't know if Tilly, Clara or even Olivia is planning to come today but someone as mean as you are can surely sit in that chair all day and night." She folded her arms across her chest and leaned against the door jamb.

"I'm sorry and I mean that. I hate being dependent on someone else for every little thing. Would you please help me?" His tone had changed drastically.

"Apology accepted." She crossed the room and with the right motion had him on his feet in only a few seconds.

"How do you do that? You're not any bigger than a bar of soap after a hard day's washin' and yet you know just what to do." He addressed her as he slowly crutched his way into the hallway and toward the bathroom.

"I was trained to take care of people like you." She let him do as much as he could but when he had to stop at the halfway point, she slipped her shoulder under his good side to give his hand a rest and became the other crutch. "I'll be right here when you finish in there. You can use the walls and the sink to brace yourself. Don't fall." She took the other crutch from him and he grabbed the door.

Fifteen minutes later he was back in his room, quite content to be wearing clean pajamas. Now he was ready for company.

"What time is it?" He asked.

She checked the watch pin on the lapel of her pale blue work dress. "Mid morning. Ten minutes past ten. Why?"

"Seems later. Thought maybe it was time for Tilly or Clara," he said.

"Lonely after only two days?" She asked.

"No, cabin fever after two days. I haven't been cooped up since we were kids and had the chicken pox and measles. I hate being in the house all day with nothing to do. Matter of fact, I hate being in the house even if I have something to do. Lonely has nothing to do with it."

"Sorry. I truly am. The morning paper is down on the porch by now. I'll bring it up. At least that will keep you occupied until lunch and maybe someone will come to visit this afternoon," she said.

"How'd the paper get on the porch?"

"One of Briar's hired hands comes by here to check some wells nearby. He comes through town and picks it up and tosses it on the porch. Briar took care of that for you."

"If he'd go over Clara's head and fire you, I'd make him sole beneficiary of all I own," Tucker said.

"Wouldn't be worth it. Clara is the love of his life, Libby's mother and besides she's about to have another baby. Your kingdom pales in comparison."

"Clara is expecting?" Tucker grinned.

"Didn't you know? Oops, I've probably spoiled it for the big announcement in the near future. If you breathe a word, I'll make your life miserable, Tucker."

"How'd you know?"

"I'm a doctor." Addison all but moaned.

"Guess I keep forgetting that part."

Her full lips tightened down into a firm line and she had to fight back the impulse to slam the bedroom door. She did give in to the urge to stomp down the steps, but the noise wasn't as satisfying as if she'd been wearing heavy work boots. Somehow, sock feet didn't make nearly enough noise.

The gray skies had started to spit a mixture of snow and sleet when she opened the front door. The dog trotted from the back yard and up on the porch. He wagged his tail and his eyes begged to come inside where it was warm. She picked up the paper, scratched his cold ears, and shut the door, but those big pleading eyes haunted her.

She opened the door. "Okay, feller, come on in. I guess—" She didn't get the sentence finished. The dog was a golden blur as he scooted up the steps and went right into Tucker's room. So much for keeping him in the kitchen on an old hook rug.

"Hey, what are you doing here?" Tucker asked.

He didn't sound too angry. She took her time taking the newspaper to him, waiting for him to begin bellowing about a dog in the house, but he didn't. When she reached his door, she leaned against the jamb, unable to believe her eyes. The dog was curled up; sound asleep at the foot of Tucker's bed.

"So he's allowed inside, I take it?" She asked.

"Of course. His name is Bill after William Shakespeare. He usually sleeps beside my bed. I should've remembered and told you. Poor old feller." Tucker rubbed his cold fur with the toes on his good foot.

"I've been feeding him scraps and eggs for breakfast," Addison said.

"That's fine. Fix double for me and give him whatever I get. That's what I usually do. Bill and I do just fine here by ourselves, don't we old man?"

"There'll come a day when you will again, I'm sure. Now you want to hold this newspaper and read it yourself or you want me to read to you?"

"I can read my own paper," his tone changed.

She wasn't surprised. Bill was part of his life. She was barely a necessary evil.

"Good, I'm going to clean the bathroom and finish the bedrooms. Planned on burning papers again today but the snow and sleet put a stop to that idea."

He didn't answer. When she turned to leave the newspaper was propped on a pillow and he was already intrigued with his reading. That was fine with her. She'd had to verbally spar with lots of patients during her internship in Little Rock, but Tucker Anderson could put them all to shame. Cleaning house seemed a small price to pay to get away from his sharp tongue for a while.

She'd barely wiped a decade worth of dust from the washstand beside the bed in one of the guestrooms when he called out to her. She sighed and considered putting a heavy dose of morphine in his tea at lunch. She wasn't surprised at his demands. She'd found that the first couple of days after a man was injured he was content to rest. After that they were worse than children.

"What do you need?" She asked at the doorway.

"Lost my paper. It's a chore to turn the pages with my left hand and my right one hurts. Would you read this to me . . . please," he said.

At least he'd learned to ask politely, even if his tone left a lot to be desired. She gathered up the pages and reorganized the paper. "Here are a couple of articles about the two new picture shows over in Ardmore. One's called 'Why Marry?' and the other one is 'Trifles.' The person who wrote this is up in arms about what kind of trash the motion picture people are putting out there on the big screen."

"Why?" Tucker asked. "I never go to the picture show. It's a waste of time."

"I love them. They take me to faraway places and for a little while I forget all about everything."

"If they're all that great, then why is someone up on a soap box about them being trash?"

"According to this, one movie is about a woman who kills her husband. Puts a rope around his neck and strangles him right there beside her in the bed and then says she doesn't know who killed him. She was sound asleep beside him when the body was discovered. The local authorities say that they can't believe a wife would ever kill her husband." Addison scanned and talked at the same time. It wasn't a far stretch of her imagination to think about Tucker's wife slipping a noose around his neck and watching his eyes pop out.

"Why would a woman ever kill her husband?" he pondered aloud, thinking of Tilly and Clara and the way they adored their men folks. "She'd have nothing."

"Maybe she had nothing when she was married to him." Addison swiftly took the other side of the debate. "Not all couples are as in love as Olivia and Julius, you know? Some men are downright mean to their wives. Maybe this man was one of those and she couldn't take anymore."

"But to kill him and then sleep beside his dead body?" He snarled his nose.

"Might be the only time she'd been happy that close to him. Maybe he beat her or was mean and hateful."

"Could you do it? Could you kill your husband and then sleep beside him?"

"We never know what we might do until we've been in the circumstances of that person."

"The old 'walk a mile in his shoes theory,' huh?"

"Something like that. This other show is about a woman who lives with her fiancé but doesn't want to marry him. That would put society on its ear, now wouldn't it? No wonder this writer, and he's a man by the way, is so up in arms. One woman kills without remorse; another is content to live with her feller without the sanction of marriage. He would think such things were abominations and the world was about to come to an end."

"Would you do that?" Tucker cocked his head off to one side. Lord save him from these new modern women. He should have let Olivia catch him, now that he had the perfect vision of hindsight. She, at least, was content to make a proper home for Julius. The man didn't know how lucky he was.

"Again, one never knows what they'd do until they walked that old proverbial mile. Would you ask a woman to live with you without marrying her?"

"I am a decent man. No, I wouldn't ask a woman to do that. Great God Almighty, Addison. That doesn't even bear thinking about. But I can see where folks would be up in arms about the industry putting such things in the pictures. It would give women ideas and Lord only knows they've got enough of them as it is. Look at you, you're a doctor! And whether us men folks like it or not, the women are going to keep on until they get the vote and then it'll be a nightmare. They'll expect to hold down men's jobs and get the same pay. They'll forsake their homes and leave their children. It'll all go to hell in a handbag for sure."

"What will? The lush life men live?"

"So you're one of those hard-headed women? I should've known since you're a doctor."

"That's right, Tucker, and I'm glad you're admitting it."

"Admitting it and accepting it are two different things," he declared. He'd never felt so alive in his life. Lying there propped up on pillows, unable to even shave his own face or take a bath, and his pulse raced, his heart slipped in a couple of extra beats, his mind raced trying to think of what she'd say next.

"It's your privilege to accept or deny anything, but it doesn't change things one bit does it? The sun will still go down in the west and come up in the east, and in a few years women will vote. You might as well accept it, Tucker, because it's coming."

"Like you say, it's my privilege. I choose to ignore it. When I marry, it'll be to a woman who'll love me so much, murder won't ever cross her mind and who wouldn't dream of wanting to live with me without a marriage license."

Addison's whole face lit up when she giggled. "There's not a woman on earth that could live with you and not think about murder."

Chapter Five

Tucker waited until he heard Addison and Bill leave the house before he swung his legs to the side of the bed, picked up his crutches and declared his independence. First he made his way to the bathroom where he slowly shaved with his left hand, leaving only two blood spots on his chin. Running a sink full of water, he sat on the toilet and proceeded to give himself a bath. Granted, he did miss the way Addison's massaging fingers felt on his back, but by damn, he'd taken care of his business without her help. He'd show the whole bunch of them that he was tough as nails.

He kicked his dirty pajamas out into the hallway and carefully redressed himself. He missed his long underwear, his flannel shirt and overalls. He missed dressing up to go to church on Sunday. He missed living. One

week down and five more to go, then he'd have his
ranch back to himself. Not that Addison hadn't done a
fair job of keeping things going. Briar and Ford both
bragged on her every time they came around. Ford had
helped a couple of times with the evening chores and
stayed to visit a spell, but Tucker could tell his mind
was on his own home where Tilly waited. It was the
same story with Briar. He visited, but his mind was on
Clara and Libby.

Tucker was still amazed that Ford and Tilly were
married. Everyone in the county knew they were made
for each other even if she was a moonshine runner and
Ford, the sheriff who was bound, damned and determined to catch her. When it all came down to the core
of the matter though, it didn't matter to their hearts if
one was on the wrong side of the law and the other was
the law. Three weeks later they still acted as if they'd
been married forever and been in love every day of it.
As Addison said about Olivia and Julius, the bloom was
still on the marriage. Someday, Tucker hoped he'd find
someone like that. A woman who'd make his heart
jump around and someone he'd rather be at home with
rather than anywhere else.

Being careful not to stumble over the dirty laundry,
he made his way into one of the bedrooms. It hadn't
looked that nice since before his mother died. The curtains were clean, starched stiff and ironed. If there was
a speck of dirt or a dust bunny hiding under the bed,
he'd eat his grungy socks for supper. He sat down in a

rocking chair for a few minutes. Lying flat on his back for a whole week had sure taken the starch out of him. A simple shave, bath and walk across the hallway and he was as limp as a used dish rag.

He pushed the curtains back and gazed, longingly, out the window. A couple of inches of snow and sleet on the ground, skies heavy enough to break open any minute and really lay a snow storm on the whole area. Addison was driving a truck loaded with hay from the garage toward the pasture. Bill's round yellow face was pressed against the passenger window. That scoundrel. He knew he was supposed to ride in the bed of the truck. He'd convinced Addison to let him inside so he wouldn't get cold.

By the time she was out of sight, he was ready to inspect the other guest room. A big oak four poster bed covered with a pink and white checkered quilt. This was where Clara liked to sleep when she came to spend the night back when they were children. She always said she was a princess when she walked into the room. He sank into the overstuffed chair beside the window facing out into the front yard and pulled back the lace curtains. No one was coming down the lane. Tilly wouldn't let a little bad weather keep her in, but she'd far rather spend her days inside with Ford than an ailing old bear of a cousin, even if he was more like her brother. Tucker wallowed around in a pity pool for a few minutes, then shook off the cabin fever and went toward his own room.

He stopped at the door and turned around. He could manage the steps if he went very slowly. At least he figured he could until he looked down them. It looked like a hundred miles to the foyer. Everything started spinning and his legs felt as if they were going to buckle beneath him. He hurriedly backed up, and attempted to get his stomach to quit flipping around. His heart thumped loud enough for Addison to hear it all the way out to the south pasture, and his hands were clammy by the time he found a chair and eased himself down into it. It wasn't until his vision cleared that he realized he was sitting in his parent's room. The one Addison had chosen for hers just because the mattress was the softest in the house.

Two trunks were thrown open but the contents were neat. A navy blue skirt had been carefully draped over the back of the ladder chair in front of the fireplace where embers were glowing crimson. A white blouse hung on the bedpost. Everything was as neat as the other rooms but there was a soft fragrance still lingering in the air. He lifted his nose slightly and inhaled. Roses. He found the bottle of rose scented perfume on the vanity beside her hair brush, mirror and comb. His grandmother, Katy, always smelled like that.

He heard the truck coming back and peeked out the window. Addison crept along. Strange, he thought, since she'd driven that morning as if it were a bright sunny day and the tires were on gravel instead of ice and snow. Then he saw the heifer coming along behind

the truck, bawling from the way she had her head
thrown back. Bill was in the back and there was something else in the cab with Addison—a calf that had
been born out of season. It would never live, especially
if it was an early birth. She drove the truck right up to
the front of the barn and went around to the passenger
door where she took off her heavy coat and wrapped it
around a calf not much bigger than Bill. She was a
tough woman, he'd give her that much. Even though
her legs looked like they'd bow with the weight, she
didn't miss a step. The cow followed Doc right into the
barn where she'd put both of them in a warm stall.

"Doc!" He snorted aloud. He might think that word
but he'd never give her the satisfaction of saying it in
her presence.

Addison grabbed a horse blanket from a nail inside
the tack room and rubbed the poor little half frozen bull
calf until it finally bawled. A faint little noise that
scarcely sounded like a hungry baby, but it was alive.
She helped it stand on wobbly legs and held it up to its
mother's udders. In a few minutes she had it sucking
contentedly. The heifer didn't argue when she shut the
gate to the stall, but seemed to be happy to be in out of
the cold with her newborn baby.

"Well, Bill, we've done a fair morning's work and
I'm about to freeze to death myself. Let's go have a cup
of good hot coffee before we give the old bear his bath
and shave him. I sure didn't know winter was going to

be this tough when I agreed to do the chores as well as take care of him."

She noticed Tilly coming up the lane when she crossed the yard. Her car with the Sweet Tilly metal plaque on the front was easy to recognize. Addison welcomed the company. She'd make coffee and pull out the chocolate cake with seven minute icing she'd made the day before. Maybe Tilly would even stay for lunch. Even though they argued, Tucker was always in a better mood when she visited.

Tilly waved and darted inside the front door before Addison made her way to the back door. By the time she'd removed her boots and freezing wet socks at the back door, she could hear Tilly and Tucker talking. She couldn't make out their words but the tone told her they were already arguing. At that moment, Addison missed her own brother. They disagreed on everything, especially her going to college and then to medical school. To his way of thinking, she should settle down when she was sixteen with the farmer on the next section line and make babies. He and Tucker would hit it right off. They thought the same, and farmed the same. Difference was that she loved Luke even if she didn't like him some days. Tucker wasn't loveable or likeable. He was just grouchy.

She filled the coffee pot with cold water and added half a cup of grounds. Luke used a whole cup of grounds. He boiled it until the pot was half full before he sampled the goods. She'd told him that was why he didn't have a wife. No one could stand his coffee. He said if it didn't curl his hair and make his eyes pop out then it wasn't anything but murdered water.

She smiled at the memory of them teasing over their coffee. She'd need to write her father and brother a note this next week. She didn't need to tell them about the deal with Magnolia. Just a short note about the weather being so cold and how much she liked the people she'd met. That would be enough.

The aroma of boiling coffee filled the kitchen while she sliced chocolate cake. She arranged the plates on the tray she carried up and down for Tucker's meals. It would be nice when he was able to manage the stairs and come to the table. She might even plan a party with Clara and Briar, Tilly and Ford. A 'finally got rid of the woman doctor' dinner when she pronounced Tucker fully healed and ready to manage his own ranch. That would be a glorious day and it would be the last time she ever tried a hitch at private practice.

What she wanted and had always wanted was her own clinic, but that took either lots of money or someone to back her. She had neither so an enlistment in the army would be her next stop. Maybe she could save all her paychecks and at least have enough to begin a practice when the war ended.

"Yeah right. Women might let me deliver babies and I'd be a glorified mid-wife. But men coming around to my clinic would be nothing short of a miracle. I'm not sure there's any miracles left, especially here in Healdton, Oklahoma."

Tilly was surprised to see Tucker's bed empty. Clothing was piled outside the bathroom and the door was open so he wasn't in there. "Tucker?" She called out cautiously. He'd been pretty docile these past few days but it couldn't last long. She just hoped he hadn't gone outside and Addy was having the devil of a time trying to get him back inside on the ice.

"In here," he said from Addison's room.

"What are you doing in here? And where's the doc? And does she know you're up on your own?" Tilly bombarded him with questions.

He used his left hand to heft himself up out of the chair and balance on the crutches. "No, she doesn't and she's downstairs making coffee if my nose isn't lying to me and I'm in here because I got dizzy when I looked down the stairs. And you're not going to tell on me, either."

"You got dizzy?" Tilly felt the color drain from her face.

"Get me back in the bed before she gets up here or she'll fuss at me all afternoon," he said.

Tilly folded her arms over her chest and glared at him. "On one condition. That you don't try to get up unless she's in the house. What on earth were you thinking? Hells bells, Tucker. If you fall down the stairs it could kill you dead."

"Guess in the back of my mind it reminded me of the fall. Scared the bejesus out of me, I tell you. Got all clammy and you don't have to worry. I won't be trying to get off this floor for a while. You want to change those sheets right quick. I can sit in the chair and she'll think that's what I'm doing up. I hear her coming."

"I'm covering up for you, but if you cross me I'll tell." Tilly jerked the sheets from the bed and was in the process of taking clean ones from the chest when Addison arrived, bearing a tray full of food.

"What are you doing up?" She eyed Tucker closely. He was pale and those were clean pajamas. She set the tray on the wash stand and grabbed her stethoscope. His heart was a little fast. Nothing too drastic considering he'd gotten out of bed himself and given himself both a bath and shave.

"I had to go to the bathroom so I used the time wisely. Shaved and bathed. Changed clothing. Tilly said she'd do up the bed for me." He avoided looking into those dark green eyes that most likely could see a lie a hundred yards away.

"You shouldn't be up with no one in the house. If you fell you'd have to lie there until I came back. If you're strong enough to take care of your bath and shave, that's fine. The exercise will do you good, but don't do it without me in the house," she said.

He didn't argue.

That meant he'd done more than just go to the bathroom and back to his room. She'd be willing to put a week's salary on it.

Tilly noticed the cake when she finished her job. "Chocolate cake! Tucker, you might as well eat it sitting up. I don't want crumbs all over the clean sheets."

"You feel like it? You look a little pale to me. Don't want you to overdo it." Addison forced him to look at her by standing right in front of him.

"Sure, I'm not tired at all."

He lied but he did it well. Not a single blink in those steely blue eyes. Not a bit of a quiver in that strong chin with two little bubbles of dried blood at the top and bottom of the cleft.

Tilly didn't need an invitation to grab the biggest chunk of cake and begin eating. "What I came for other than to see this sorry rascal and make sure you hadn't killed him, was to tell you we've got a poetry reading tomorrow night. I'll pick you up if you'd like to go and Ford has offered to stay with the patient here. I expect they can play poker or tell tall tales. It'll give you a break. We'll have supper at the Morning Glory with Beulah and Dulcie before so don't eat. Make the old bear here a sandwich or something light."

"Thanks a lot." Tucker ate cake and sipped good coffee. He'd miss three meals brought to him every day when Addison was gone. But that's all he'd miss. Her sass and bossiness would be more than welcome to scoot right on out of the county.

"Poetry reading?" Addison asked.

"Yes, tomorrow night we're reading Shakespeare. You won't have to read, just be a visitor. There's half a dozen of us on a good night. We read and discuss. Have refreshments and visit a while. Clara and I started it when we were still in high school in one of our save the cultural world days. Tucker had to escort us into town in those days because it wasn't proper for young ladies to be out after dark alone. By the time we got to be old maids, it was just habit for him to tag along. This will be the first one he's ever missed."

"Who says I'm not going?" He asked.

"I do," Tilly and Addison said in perfect unison.

"Can't fight the system but someday I'll be well and I'm kicking both of you out. Now, you reckon you could move over so I can stretch this leg back out on that bed?"

Addison's first thought was a smart retort about how he wasn't as tough as he'd professed when he wanted to run the whole ranch with a broken leg. However, she wanted to know more about the poetry reading so she held her tongue, knowing that her remark would bring on a full-fledged argument about how he was mean enough to whip a grizzly with a toothache with his bare fists.

"So tell me more about the poetry thing." She slipped the top sheet up to Tucker's waist and fluffed another pillow for his back.

"Folks about town call it the Dreamer's Club. We

had some fancy name for it in the beginning but no one, not even Clara, remembers what it is. We're just the Dreamer's now."

"I'd love to go." Addison looked forward to the diversion.

"Good, then I'll pick you up at a quarter 'til five. Dulcie said supper is at five and the meeting starts at six."

"But the evening chores? I'm sorry. I won't have them done by then. I'll have to stay in." Addison's heart fell. For that moment she envisioned a room full of women to visit with and even though it was short-lived, she was terribly disappointed.

"Oh, no, you don't. You can't back out. Ford and Briar will take care of the evening jobs. You deserve a night out after a week with this feller," she said.

Addison could have hugged her on the spot. "Thank you."

Tucker narrowed his eyes. "So what makes me so hard to get along with? Haven't I been the model patient? I've let you shave me when I was scared you'd slit my throat. I even cut up my new pair of long johns without too much fuss."

"Oh, yes, darlin', I'm sure you've been so good that Doc wishes she had a whole house full of patients just like you," Tilly laughed.

Addison couldn't remember the last time she'd eaten a meal she hadn't prepared. Other than the few times she forced a few bites down on the trip from east

Arkansas to Healdton. When she was home she cooked. When she was in school she had a small hot plate in her room where she fixed her meals.

"This is wonderful," she told Beulah.

"I didn't cook. Dulcie did. She's the best cook in the whole state, and her hot chicken casserole can't be beat. I think it's because she starts with fresh chicken and boils it slow so there's good broth for the sauce. She's been at the Morning Glory Inn since before it was an inn. Clara's mother didn't like to cook any better than Clara does, so they hired Dulcie even before Clara was born. I tell her she squatted on a grassy lot and they built the inn around her."

Dulcie laughed and all three chins jiggled. "Might be the truth. Ain't regretted working here one day of my life, either, but these old bones is gettin' tired. One of these days I'm goin' to quit."

"So your parents aren't living any more?" Addison asked Clara.

"No. All three of us lost our parents. Tilly's in the Houston Hurricane when she wasn't very old. Granny Anderson raised her. My father died and my mother turned this house into the Morning Glory Inn. Tucker's mother died when he was young and his father a few years ago. Beulah and Bessie stepped in, along with Dulcie, and kept us in line though. Even if Dulcie did make a big mistake a few months ago and rented a room to one of those horrible oil men." Clara's crystal blue eyes twinkled.

"Who says it was a mistake?" Dulcie teased. "Got you a good husband and a daughter out of the deal. I'd say I did right good. Might be the last good thing I do before I stop this job."

"Why are you talking about quitting so much tonight?" Tilly asked.

"Just gettin' y'all prepared for the day when Dulcie ain't going to be here anymore. Don't want you to be surprised."

"What would you do without Dulcie, Beulah?" Clara asked.

"I might be forced to quit, too," Beulah winked at Dulcie but Addison saw it.

"Well, that's enough of that kind of conversation," Cornelia said. "What would us old maid schoolteachers do without a good boarding house?"

Nellie blew out. "Hmmph. You won't be an old maid much longer. You and George are just waiting for the divorce to be final before you tie the knot. I'm the old maid schoolteacher here and I'll be giving notice soon."

"Things are changing," Beulah said.

"Started when Dulcie let that oil man in here," Nellie said.

"Yes, and it'll end just fine. Now it's time for you girls to get on down to the Dreamer's meeting. You'll be lost without Tucker," Beulah said.

But they weren't.

They read. They discussed. And Addison scarcely could believe the evening had passed so fast. She'd fallen in love with Beulah and Dulcie. She'd made friends with Cornelia, who was going to marry the druggist, George Simpson. Seems his wife had run away with an oil man not long ago and Cornelia helped him out in the drug store when she wasn't teaching. She'd gotten to know Nellie who had a sharp tongue and could use anything for a soap box when it came to women's rights. Olivia had been there even though she said she hated poetry and only came for the fun and socializing. Libby, Clara's daughter, had stolen her heart.

That night when she'd told Tucker everything she could remember about the evening and he was sleeping soundly, she sat in the rocking chair in her room and decided maybe she'd been too hasty in her first impression of the small town. It had some fine people in it.

Chapter Six

"I'm going to be the first man to ever die of an itching leg," Tucker groused.

Addison was pleased with her patient. He was able to get himself out of bed and wander all over the upstairs. Before long he'd be demanding to go to the ground floor. Once the stitches were out of his hand and he could get a firm grip on the crutches, he'd master that, too. Even if his attitude was rough as sandpaper most of the time, he was mending beautifully. If she'd been cooped up inside for almost two weeks, she'd probably be worse than he'd been.

"Did you hear me?" Tucker asked.

"I heard you. It's a common malady with a broken limb. The skin gets flaky under the cast and itches. It's not fatal even if it isn't pleasant. Morning paper is right here." She pointed to the table beside his rocking chair. "Pillow where you can reach it so you can spread it out." She talked as she remade his bed. These days he seldom got back into it during the day. He spent his time in the chair: reading, staring forlornly out the window, visiting with Clara or Tilly in the afternoon and grumbling about not being able to go outside.

"There is something you can do about it. Doesn't bring lots of relief but it's better than nothing," she told him.

"I sure can't reach inside there and scratch and that's what I want to do. Found myself digging at the cast during the night. When I woke, my fingernail was broken and it was still itching," he said.

She glanced around the room. Not a single fly swatter in sight, but there was one in the kitchen on a nail beside the back door.

"I'll be right back. Need anything else?"

"Just your miracle drug and maybe for the next four weeks to pass quickly."

"One I can produce. The other is out of my league. I think that's beyond a miracle and is only discussed briefly in the magic chapter of the medical book." She whistled as she left the room.

How on earth could a sane person be happy when his leg itched so badly? The whistling got fainter and fainter then suddenly it began to get louder. He'd learned her step on the stairs. When she cleaned the first floor of the house he knew exactly what room she

was in and how many trips she made out the back door
burning the mountains of newspapers. He wondered if
the other parts of the house were as spotless as the upstairs section. Sometimes he wandered through the two
unused bedrooms and simply soaked up the aura there.
They reminded him so much of the time when his
mother was still alive. There were days when Addison
was cleaning that he could shut his eyes and remember
hearing his mother whistling or humming as she did
her chores. He couldn't wait until he was well enough
to make the trip to the living room, the dining room, the
kitchen and just see what it all looked like these days.
That might not happen until his leg was fully healed
since he broke out in a cold sweat every time he looked
down. He could still remember the helpless feeling in
that instant before he fell.

"Found the miracle drug." She held up a fly swatter.

One of the twelve he'd sent for a few years ago. Ten
cents each or a dollar a dozen. They'd been worth fifty
dollars a dozen. The theory behind the simple invention
was that a fly could sense a solid object coming at it and
flew before a person's hand could kill it. The screen
wire attached to the end of a smooth round stick let the
air flow through it and the fly didn't know it was approaching. Whatever the concept, they worked. And one
did not argue with an invention that produced dead flies.

"A swatter. How is that going to heal my itch?" He
frowned.

"Your leg has stopped swelling so there's a little

room in the cast," she explained. "These things are wonderful . . ."

"So what? Smearing dead flies' remains on my cast won't stop itching, will it?"

"No but shoving this handle down to the spot that's driving you crazy and using it to scratch will bring a lot of relief." She held it out.

He took it and did just what she said, a sigh escaping his lips in moments. "I wish I'd have bought ten dozen now. I think this is the last one left. I'll guard it with my life until I can get some more. This is wonderful."

"The old bear has finally been nice. I'm going to work on the dining room a little more today while the sun is shining. I want to rewash the windows and burn a few more of those papers. What on earth were you thinking, letting them pile up that way?"

He kept a steady rhythm going with the rounded end of the swatter. "Habit. Dad read them in the evening and kept a stack beside his chair. About a month's worth could be kept there before the pile got to the top of the arm and then I'd haul them up to one of the un-used bedrooms. When there wasn't space anymore, I'd just put them wherever there was a corner."

"Men!" She huffed.

"Women!" He snapped right back.

"I'm going to wash windows . . . on the inside any-way. It's too cold to do anything outside." She wasn't whistling when she left.

Even without a woman two men could surely see

what a mess all those papers created. Already the house was taking on a personality, almost as if it could breathe without the weight of so much trash everywhere. Sunlight poured into clean windows. Wooden table tops glowed without an inch of dust covering them. Next spring she'd plant morning glories around the front porch and lantana in the pitiful looking flower beds.

"Whoa!" She stopped in her tracks in the foyer. Where had that notion come from? She would be in France or Germany next spring, caring for injured soldiers, not planting flowers. Four more weeks and she'd have no choice but to leave. Suddenly, her heart fell like a heavy weight in her chest. Just like she'd been taught not to do, she'd become emotionally involved. Maybe not with Tucker Anderson, but with the Evening Star ranch. It was exactly what she'd always wanted. A big old rambling two story house with enough land around it to run cattle and have a huge vegetable garden. She wanted the whole pie: a home she could be proud of, a clinic or hospital for her patients, children to make her laugh, and a husband who adored her. None of it was up for grabs at Evening Star so she'd better back right out of that insane notion.

"I'm going to scratch to my heart's content," Tucker declared.

If she never did another good thing, he'd always be in Addison's debt for thinking of the fly swatter. He pulled the handle from the inside of the cast and stared at it, another place beginning to itch so far down in his heart that he could never scratch it. Not with a fly swatter or anything else. Something nagged him, made his heart heavy. Four more weeks and she'd be gone for good. Off to repair broken bodies from the war and he didn't want her to go. Now that was downright stupid thinking. It was just cabin fever taking over his good sense. When he could get outside and do his own work, drive his truck into town once a day to talk to Briar and stop back by Tilly's place to see how Ford was doing, then he'd be all right again. The idea would go away as quickly as it had appeared.

"You're looking serious today." Clara said from the doorway.

"I didn't hear you," he confessed, still amazed at the idea of not wanting Addison to leave Healdton.

"Evidently not. Whatever were you thinking?" She removed her coat and draped it over the footboard.

"Nothing much," he said.

"Uncle Tucker, Uncle Tucker." Libby came running through the door, black curls bouncing, blue eyes twinkling.

Anyone who saw Libby with Clara would swear she'd given birth to the child; she looked so much like Clara. Truth was that she belonged to one of the biggest film stars in all of California. Briar had married her in New York when she was big in the theater. The marriage had barely lasted long enough to produce Libby before it crumbled. She left Briar to raise the child alone while she went in search of more fame and fortune.

"Libby, I was hoping you might come to see me today." Tucker opened his arms and Libby flew into them, crawling up on his good leg and giving him a big kiss on the cheek.

"It's cold outside and my baby kittens had to come in the kitchen last night to keep from freezing. Daddy said they could stay in the kitchen behind the stove if they were good so I've been singing to them all morning so they won't be bad and guess what, Uncle Tucker, it's not snowing today and there wasn't enough to make ice cream yesterday even if we scraped it all up all the way to town."

She sucked in another lungful of air, "and Momma is teaching me to play the piano and I can already stretch my fingers this far," she held up her four and a half year old delicate hand to show him, "and when I get to be a big girl I'm going to play at church Olivia said I could and Julius said I might be a preacher someday but that's silly girls don't get to be preachers," she inhaled deeply again, "Momma says that someday girls can be preachers but they can't be preachers now. Where is Bill?" She stopped finally and looked around.

"He's out in the barn with the new baby calf. It's not much bigger than he is and he wants to stay out there. Barely can get him to come in to eat. I've got a feeling Addison has been taking his food to him. She says he sleeps right in front of the stall where the calf and its momma are. He must think they need protecting."

"From what? Would a coyote get in there and hurt that new baby calf? Can I go see it? Momma, I didn't take my coat off yet, can I go see the baby calf, please? I'll be good and not get too close I won't even touch it."

"I'll take her out if you don't mind," Addison said from the doorway. "I brought hot peppermint tea and sugar cookies."

"Bless you. That sounds wonderful," Clara said.

"I thought it might," Addison said.

The tea would calm Clara's stomach and the sugar cookies would put something down there without overloading it. It wouldn't be much longer until the sickness would pass, but Clara looked thinner and paler every time Addison saw her.

"Then I can go please Momma I'll be good and not get in Doc's way and maybe Doc can come and see my kittens tonight do you think she can?"

"Whew!" Tucker wiped at his brow. "You can ask more questions in a minute than a poor old uncle or momma can answer in a whole day."

Peppermint tea and bland old sugar cookies for a midmorning snack? Addison could do better than that. He would have rather had a chunk of pecan pie she'd baked yesterday and some good strong coffee.

"Really Uncle Tucker can I really? Come on Doc, let's go see that calf. Is it big as one of my kittens can I hold it in my hand why is it so little?" She took Addison's hand and led her away from the room.

Clara sipped the warm tea. "So you still grumpy?"

"Yes, I am and rightly so. I might be grouchy until spring after the stunt you two pulled on me."

"She's good isn't she? I haven't seen this place look this nice in years and years. Amazing what a little cleaning will do. Briar says she's a natural out there on the ranch. That calf in the barn wouldn't have made it if she hadn't been on her toes. She's not much for size, but she's sure a hard worker and a damn good doctor."

"Did I just hear a swear word escape your lips?" Tucker teased.

"You did and I think you need to tell Doc how much you appreciate all she's doing once in a while."

"She's getting paid a fortune. I don't think she's got to have praise too," he argued.

Clara rolled her blue eyes and brushed back a strand of black hair from her cheek. "You have been an old bachelor too long, Tucker Anderson. When you are well, I'm going to flood this house with eligible women and you are going to be married by Christmas. That gives you eleven months and a few days. If you aren't engaged by then, Tilly and I are going to pick a wife for you."

"I don't believe in arranged marriages," he said.

"Then you'd best find a wife. Two more years and you'll be so set in your ways, no one will have you. I swear you're as ornery as Grandpa some days."

"Nobody is that bad."

"Look in the mirror. You've got his eyes more than us girls and Lord knows you're tall and muscled up like he was. Time ain't settin' still, Tucker. You better find someone or I swear I will."

"Now listen, just because you and Tilly are all happy and glowing with this marriage thing, doesn't mean it's for me." He threw up his left hand in defense. Trying to ward off the evil marriage bug she was throwing out into his bedroom.

"Well, it's going to be. We'll have to hurry because once Doc leaves, the house will go back to ruin and no good woman wants a slob for a husband."

"Hmmph!" He sipped his peppermint tea and ignored her.

"Momma, guess what that baby calf is bigger than my kittens but Doc let me pet him and his momma didn't even care and I want one like him can we see if Daddy can make one of his cows get us one?" Libby exploded into the room like a blast of sunshine on a cloudy day.

"I'm about to start lunch. Y'all want to stay with us?" Addison asked from the doorway. Falling in love with Libby wouldn't be a difficult task. The girl was a picture of health and full of life, bringing happiness with her everywhere she went.

Libby bounced from the side of the bed to his chair and wrapped her arms around his neck. "We promised Daddy we'd come to town and go have dinner with him at the hotel today so we can't stay and I want to see if he can make his cows get me a little bitty baby calf like yours so we have to go give me a hug Uncle Tucker. You be nice to Doc she's takin' good care of that baby out there in the barn just like she takes good care of you Julius says she's an angel but I looked and she hasn't got any wings."

"You got that right." Tucker grinned.

"You know what else?" Libby cupped her hand over her mouth, putting it close to his ear.

He barely shook his head.

"There ain't one of them round things on her head neither I looked while she was pettin' the baby and there's just red hair on her head," she whispered.

"I figured as much," Tucker whispered back.

"You think about what I said. Eleven months. That's long enough," Clara said when she reached for her coat.

"Ain't goin' to happen," he said.

"What?" Addison asked.

"It's a secret," Clara winked.

Libby pulled Addison's hand and motioned for her to come closer. She whispered into her ear, "Momma says she can't keep secrets from me so I'll find out and tell you next time we come over to see Uncle Tucker."

Addison smiled and nodded.

Tucker looked at her long and hard. She barely came up to his shoulder which was a drawback in his books. He'd always envisioned a tall beautiful woman like his mother. One with blue eyes and blonde hair that cascaded down her back when she brushed it at night. Addison Carter's hair looked like she was born with the wrong color skin. It was a dark burgundy and kinked from the scalp all the way to the ends. He couldn't imagine her brushing it at night. There were twenty-eight freckles across her nose. He'd counted them while she made the bed each morning. None ever disappeared but at least there were no new ones. He liked a clear complexion. Preferably pale with just the right amount of pink on the cheek lines. Her eyes were a deep mossy green, serious most of the time but when she laughed they twinkled. Not one thing about the woman that would make him wish she wouldn't go. It must have been a passing idiotic idea spawned from an acute case of boredom.

"So what's for lunch?" He asked.

"Pot roast, potatoes, carrots, biscuits, last night's pecan pie," she rattled.

To get Evening Star she'd have to be willing to take Tucker Anderson. He was easy on the eyes with that jet black hair and those steely blue eyes but she couldn't imagine living with him. They'd kill each other before the first child came along. No, she'd forget about the house she'd fallen in love with and go on to war. At least she'd be fixing up patients, not murdering one.

"Sounds good. Will you bring your food and eat with me today?"

"I can but I'd planned to grab a quick lunch and finish cleaning the dining room. Got a little behind with

Libby's visit but I couldn't refuse that child a thing. I guess if she wanted me to sprout wings and fly, I'd attempt it."

"That's the way we all feel about her. Been like that from the first time Briar brought her to church. The dining room can wait. I'm bored out of my mind."

"And even a woman doctor beats loneliness, huh?"

"That's right," he said and wished he could learn to curb his tongue around her.

"I'll eat with you. I like honesty," she giggled.

"I thought all women liked peace."

"I'd rather have a rousting good fight with honesty at the core of it than smoldering fake peace, Mr. Anderson. So if you've got something to say, then feel free to say it. But remember I'm just as honest as you are," she said.

Chapter Seven

Addison unwrapped the bandage from Tucker's hand carefully. The wound had healed far better than she'd hoped. She picked up a pair of tiny scissors from the table she'd set beside Tucker's rocking chair. "Looks like it crossed your lifeline right in the middle but other than making a mess of a fortune teller's job, it's going to be fine."

"What are you talking about? Fortune teller?" Tucker watched as she snipped six times and pulled as many spidery looking stitches from his palm.

"This is your lifeline. See it goes from here to here. The cut on your hand splits it in the middle and the scar will make a bit of a cross out of the line. Looks like you've not lived half your life yet since there's more line on the living side of the line than on the already lived side."

"You are a gypsy?" He held his right hand up to see a fine red line where a gaping wound had been.

"No, but in medical school I roomed with a girl who believed in all that. We were the only two women in the school so we formed a friendship. You need to start using that hand now so it won't be stiff. Not digging ditches or slinging hay, but eating, combing your hair, normal everyday things. In a few days the red will start to fade. Before long you'll just have a white scar that blends in with the rest of the lines on you hand."

"What was it like, fighting your way through a man's education?" He kept staring at the lines below and above the scar. It was as if the accident did cut his life in two separate halves.

"At first Edna and I put up with a lot from the guys. Snide remarks. Crudeness. All of it. They thought they'd run us off the first semester, but they didn't. We talked about it and decided that we'd be the smartest in the class. She was the valedictorian when we graduated. I was the salutatorian. They respected us by then, even if they didn't accept us. We both were fortunate enough to intern in Little Rock. When we finished she went home to Roanoke, Virginia to set up her own practice. You know what happened to me."

Part of Tucker wanted to say, "I told you so. You don't belong in a man's world." The other part wanted to chase down every doctor who'd made Addison's life miserable and flatten his nose. It was the second part that both scared and bewildered him.

"Are you really going to join the army and go to the war?" he asked.

"Not many choices other than that, is there?"

"You could stay here," Tilly said from the doorway.

"Hey, good morning; we didn't hear you come in," Addison said.

"Parked out back and came in the kitchen door. Took my boots off at the door. They were muddy. All this rain we've had might stop the drought but it sure plays havoc with a nice clean floor." She held up one foot to show that she was in her socks.

"And you could stay here. I wasn't just talking on the spur of the moment. Ford and I've been talking about it just this morning. Healdton needs a doctor badly. It's twenty-three miles to Ardmore. I'm selfish. Even though Clara hasn't announced it yet, it doesn't mean I'm blind. She's expecting a baby and that twenty-three miles terrifies me. She's not a spring chicken. If this was her sixth or tenth child at the age of thirty, it wouldn't be any big deal, but it's her first and I'd feel better if there was a doctor right close."

Tucker held his breath. A woman doctor in Healdton. One his family would use. He'd have to swallow so much pride it would gag him. Not to mention all the words that would come back to haunt him.

Addison pointed across the hall. "I've got a trunk full

of my own supplies in there but it's scarcely enough to start a practice. I appreciate your trust in me, Tilly. I really do, but it's just not possible."

"What would it take to make it possible?" Tilly asked.

"A building for a clinic or small hospital. Equipment. Acceptance. All the fancy machinery and medicine in today's modern world wouldn't be worth much if the patients would rather die than come to me. I don't think Healdton is ready for a lady doctor. If the oil company snarls their nose at me, and even Tucker here would rather be crippled as have me take care of him, what's the attitude of the rest of the area? Just won't work, but I do thank you. Now you visit with the patient and make him laugh. Take a look at his hand. It's looking good. I've got breakfast dishes and some dusting to do."

"Why didn't you say a word?" Tilly shot Tucker a mean look as she pulled up a straight-backed chair and sat in front of him.

"What could I say? I don't think women ought to be doctors. That's a fact, Tilly. She's done a good job but I still think a woman's place is in the home, not out working. It'll bring ruination to the world, the way women are so set in taking their own way."

"You are such an opinionated fool. I'd have thought you would have changed your mind. Hell's bells, man, she's taken care of this ranch, cleaned this house until it looks like real people live here instead of hogs and wild animals. Plus she's put up with the likes of you and that alone should put a halo above her head," Tilly said.

"I know. I know. She's an angel in disguise. It's a wonder to me you all talked God into letting her leave Heaven's glory and float down here to take care of a devil like me."

Tilly threw back her head and laughed. So Addison was getting under his skin. Wasn't that just the best news in a lifetime? Addison Carter was as far from anything Tucker ever wanted as a pig's snout was from a silk purse. As far as Sheriff Ford Sloan was from Matilda Jane Anderson, the moonshine runner in Carter County, Oklahoma. Or Briar Nelson, the oil man, was from Clara Anderson, the oddball who hated all things that even smelled faintly of the oil boom. God certainly did have a sense of humor. Tilly's light blue eyes sparkled in merriment. What was it Addison said she'd need to stay in Healdton? Money could buy most of it and a few words here and there would provide the rest. Oh, yes, Tucker was about to see his worst nightmare turn into the dream of a lifetime.

"What are you laughing about?" He asked.

"You made a joke. After two weeks cooped up with a woman doctor and you made a joke. Don't be telling me everything is so terrible."

Addison had just dried the last coffee cup when she heard a vehicle approaching. The cold gravel crunched under the wheels and the engine made enough noise to stop the hens from laying for a week. "Julius," she mumbled. Clara had told her the day before that the church had voted to buy him a car so he could visit the sick and get to his Sunday afternoon church services in Wirt more comfortably in the cold weather. But they'd bought a used one that sounded like a threshing machine in need of oil. He and Olivia were as pleased with it as if it had been a brand new one straight from the dealer's showroom.

She had the back door open before they knocked, already tickled to see Olivia and hoping she planned to stay while Julius went to visit the sick and elderly. "Good morning. Come right in. Hang your coats on those hooks. I'll make a fresh pot of coffee or tea. Which would you prefer?"

"Can't stay," Julius said. "Granny Roberts is dying again. Olivia thought she'd stay with you."

"Dying? Is there anything I could do?" Addison asked.

"Never know. She gets this notion she's dying about once a month. Goes to bed and I go out there to pray her into heaven. That's what she wants. A preacher to pray over her soul as she takes her last breath. Usually we all just sit around in her room for an hour and then she declares God has told her that she's not going to pass this time. Who knows though, this could be the time."

"I'm going with you," Addison declared.

"I'll stay with Tucker then and keep him company. What have you planned for dinner? I'll have it ready when you get back." Olivia removed her coat, picked an apron from another row of hooks, and tied it around her waist.

Addison pointed at the Kelvinator as she passed it.

"There're pork chops in there. I'll get my bag and we'll see what we can do for the lady. Give me a minute."

Julius and Addison spoke very little on the drive from Evening Star to the Robert's ranch barely two miles away. A man and two grown sons waiting on the porch ushered the doctor and the preacher right into the living room where a fireplace blaze kept everything toasty warm. Soft pink rose wallpaper covered the walls, the stuffed velvet furniture invited family and friends to sit and talk a while, the kitchen and dining room were both visible and the curtains drawn to let in the sunlight. A pleasant place with no smell of death lingering in the air.

"So how is she? Are we in time?" Julius asked the eldest son, Lonny, who'd been sent to tell him to come quickly.

The young man eyed Addison. "She's still alive and asking for you. This isn't your wife. Where's Olivia?"

"This is Dr. Addison Carter and she's going to have a look at Granny this morning. See if she can figure out the cause of her illness." Julius talked as he crossed the living room and opened a door into a bedroom. "Come along Doc. Let's see what you think."

"I didn't call for no doctor." Mr. Robert's tone dripped icicles.

"There's no charge." Addison had dealt with his kind before.

"I don't take charity." His chin raised two inches and he looked down his nose at her.

"You got chickens?" She asked.

"Of course, we have chickens," Mrs. Roberts said.

"Then I'll take two dozen eggs. We're out over at the Evening Star and I'd like to make an angel food cake this week." Addison bargained.

"Done." Mrs. Roberts held out her hand.

Addison shook it to complete the deal.

"Julius, this time the Lord is calling me home. I can hear Cyrus' voice telling me it's time for me to join him." Granny fluttered her eyes.

Addison noticed the lump under the quilt was good sized. Her face was pink and healthy looking. Her hair was salted with a dose of gray but the braid hanging over her shoulder was a good two inches thick. The curtains were drawn, blocking out the light. Everything was clean if a bit sterile looking. Rather cold, and not weatherwise.

"This is Doctor Addison Carter. She's come to check you. Maybe find out what is ailing you," Julius explained.

"I ain't never been to a doctor in my whole life and don't need one now." Granny's eyelids snapped open.

"Well, she's come all this way," Julius said.

"Then she can go all the way back," Granny told him.

Addison set her bag on the floor beside the bed and opened it. "I'd like a few minutes alone with this lady. Your son has already paid the bill for me to check you so you might as well let me. What's your first name, ma'am?"

"It's Sally and my son shouldn't have paid you. Go away. How'd a woman get to be a doctor anyway?"

Addison took out a stethoscope and stuck it in her ears. She pulled the covers back to find a big, healthy woman. "I went to school just like men do. Only I was smarter than any of them and beat them all when it came to learning. I'm going to listen to your heart."

"So you were smarter than the men, were you?" Sally smiled.

Her teeth were small but still intact, healthy-looking gums. Addison listened intently, counting beats. Strong. Healthy. That heart was not going to give up the ghost in the next five minutes for sure.

"Yes, ma'am. Showed them all up. Came out second in the class and guess what? The top student was the only other woman in the graduating class."

"Good for you. Did my son pay you enough to give me a good going over? I ain't never been to a doctor in my life. Don't expect it would hurt to have a good check-up if it's already paid for." Sally's tone was anything but weak and dying.

"Yes, he paid me double and I'll be glad to take a look at you. Sit up here and swing your legs over the bed," Addison said.

Sally did as she was told and Addison checked her reflexes. "How old would you be on your next birthday, Sally?"

"Ain't polite to ask a woman her age, but if it'll stay in this room, I'll be seventy. I don't expect to see it though. I'd just as soon die and go on to eternity with Cyrus."

"Cyrus would be your late husband?"

"That's right. Married to him more'n fifty years. Good hard working man, and I was just as hardworkin'. Right up to the day they laid him in the ground and I let this mollycoddlin' bunch bring me here to live. Might as well be dead."

"Could you walk over to the end of the room and back for me?" Addison asked.

"I could walk all the way from here to heaven, right up them stairs and all." She hopped out of bed and practically ran to the end of the room and back.

No short-windedness. Only a slight limp in her left leg.

"Got a little arthritis there?" Addison asked.

"Old Arthur visits me from time to time. Never kept me from doing my work, though, not 'til I come here." She tilted her chin up defiantly.

So that's where the son got the mannerism.

"Now I want you to sit on the edge of this bed and tell me what you do all day long so I'll be able to understand why you are dying." Addison sat down in a rocker beside the window and waited.

"Nothing. Not one durn thing. I wake up and think, 'Dammit, another day and I didn't die in the night,' and then I just lay here. I hear them out there, talkin' and laughin', and all. But I have to wait 'til they bring my breakfast to the bed on a tray. Then I get up and sit in the rocker you're settin' in 'til lunch. I go to the table and eat and sit in the rocker in front of the fireplace 'til supper. Then I go to bed and hope I die."

"I see. I think I can make you well, Sally." She stuck her head out the bedroom door and asked if Mr. and Mrs. Roberts would join them.

"Is she?" Mrs. Roberts raised an eyebrow.

"Not anytime soon," Addison said.

"I've diagnosed her problem. It's going to take some doing to make her well again and I need your help. Mrs. Roberts, could you use some help running this house?"

"Of course, I could. Got two big strapping boys and a husband at home, two grown daughters, and two sons who're all married with kids that come on Sunday for the whole day. But this isn't about me. It's about Mother and her health." Mrs. Roberts pushed a long strand of honey blonde hair back into the bun at the nape of her neck. Her round face was cheery enough but worry wrinkles creased her forehead and eyes.

"I want Sally to get out of bed when she awakes in the morning and if no one else is up, she's going to start the coffee brewing and make the biscuits for breakfast. That will keep her fingers nimble and arthritis won't set in. After breakfast which she'll take at the kitchen table with the family, she's to have one BC powder. Sitting at the table will keep her legs from getting in bad shape where she can't walk. Then I want her to sweep the entire front room and make her bed, clean up her room. When the weather is fit, she's to sweep the porch, too. Fresh air will be good for her. She is to help prepare lunch and if you take it to the men in the field in the spring and summer, she can go with you. Walking will be good for her joints."

"But, she's old and we have to pamper her," Lonny said.

"I'm not old. You paid this woman doctor to cure me, now let her do her job." Sally folded her hands over her ample bosom and set her jaw.

Addison went on, "In the afternoon, after lunch is served and she will help with the dishes, she needs to sit in the rocker before the fire for one hour in the winter or on the porch in the summer, but I want her to have mending in her hands or crochet or needlework of some kind to keep her fingers nimble. After that, Mrs. Roberts, she can help you with whatever you need. Maybe she could prepare supper and leave you free to take care of other farm business. Do you have any moonshine on the place?"

The boys looked at their feet. Mrs. Roberts blushed. Mr. Roberts cleared his throat. Julius bit his lip to keep from laughing aloud.

"Julius, shut your ears and don't blow that part about judging out of the Bible," Addison said.

"We keep a pint jar in the kitchen for medicine. Does a fine job of curing a sore throat," Mrs. Roberts said.

"Good. I want you to brew a cup of hot tea each evening. Hot as Sally can stand to drink it. Put one teaspoon of sugar or honey it in and one teaspoon of moonshine. She's to drink it sitting in her rocking chair in her bedroom and then go straight to bed for the evening. Also, Sally, I want you to go to church on Sunday morning with the family. If you miss a Sunday, Julius is going to tell me and I'll be out here to see why you're sick. Is that understood?"

"I ain't never drank a drop of liquor in my life and I ain't startin' now," Sally huffed.

"You want to live to see these boys full grown and married?" Addison asked.

"It was Cyrus' fondest wish for us to see the boys grown. I guess since he can't I should."

"Then do as I say," Addison said. "Understood?"

"Yes," Sally nodded seriously. "It's midmorning, ain't it? Time for me to help make lunch for this bunch of wild men. How many potatoes you think we need to peel, Lizzy?" She winked at Addison and looked at her daughter-in-law.

"You sure about this? We just wanted her to live her last years in comfort with all of us waiting on her hand and foot," Lizzy said.

"You paid the woman. Listen to her. Now get out of my room and let me get dressed. I ain't never peeled potatoes in my nightgown before and that's one thing I ain't startin' now. Lizzy, have them boys bring my boxes from the shed. I want to put out a few things in this room. Fix it up like it was mine and Cyrus' room. I can do that after I do the mendin' this afternoon." Sally was already out of bed and searching through the armoire for a dress.

"You sure this will keep her alive?" Lizzy walked Julius and Addison out on the porch. She wrapped a woolen shawl tightly around her shoulders.

"How well do you get along with her?" Addison asked.

"Never had a complaint until she moved in with us and started dying every few weeks. And Lord knows I could use the help if you think it won't hurt her."

"She needs to be needed. Just do what I said for a week and you'll have your old mother-in-law back," Addison said.

"I'd try anything." Lizzy waved at them.

"How did you do that?" Julius asked as they drove toward the Evening Star. "And why did you prescribe BC Powder and whiskey?"

"She's got a little bit of a limp. The powder will keep down the pain. A teaspoon of whiskey isn't going to do much but, along with the hot tea, it will make her sleep better and stop thinking about dying. Going to church will put her in company with other women her age and get her out of the house once a week. Basically the hot tea is to help the rest of the family think they're doing something for her. Pampering her, if you please. Can't take it all away from them and give it all to Sally."

"How'd you get to be so wise?" Julius asked.

"I've been to college," she said with a smile.

They opened the door into the kitchen and were greeted with the wonderful aroma of bread baking, pork chops frying and green beans simmering in onions. Potatoes were ready to be mashed and Olivia had everything under control.

Tucker heard the car and hobbled across the hall to look out the window of one of the spare rooms. Addison carried her bag. Julius talked but Tucker couldn't hear what he said. Evidently they'd pulled Granny Roberts out of death's grasp one more time because neither of them looked too sad. That's all he needed! For the town folks to begin to think of Addison as a doctor. She might wedge a foot in the door and decide to stay. He could wring Tilly's neck for suggesting such a thing. Now the seed would be planted in Addison's mind and what would he do if it grew?

He positioned his crutches better under his arms and made his way to the top of the stairs, staying back two feet and looking down over the banister. It was still three miles to the bottom. A fine bead of sweat covered his upper lip and his hands were so clammy, he feared he wouldn't be able to grip the handles of his crutches. He balanced on his left leg and wiped his hand on his pajamas, then very carefully went back to his room, wondering if he'd ever be able to actually walk down those stairs without a panic attack.

"Hey, guess what," Olivia said a few minutes later when she carried his lunch into the room. "Doc cured Granny Roberts."

"How'd she do that?" Tucker asked.

"With BC Powder, moonshine and hard work," Julius said right behind Olivia.

Addison set the tray she carried on the floor. "Thought we'd have a picnic in here with you so you won't have to eat alone."

Tucker listened to the story while he ate. Addison was a genius; he'd have to admit that much. Granny Roberts had worked hard her entire life. To be put out to pasture would be signing her death certificate.

"She's more than a doctor. She's a—" Olivia searched for the right word.

"Woman," Addison completed the sentence.

She didn't think she could stand being called an angel again. If these people knew how ornery she'd been her whole life they'd be dodging lightning bolts for even thinking such a thing.

"Just a woman who saw what the problem was and a doctor who thought Sally needed a little bit of pain medicine once a day. She might not have taken it for the family but since she wasn't about to waste the price they paid me to treat her, she will for me."

"What did you charge them?" Tucker asked.

"Two dozen eggs. Oh, my, Julius, we'll have to bring them in or they'll freeze and crack," she said.

"Pretty steep prices," Tucker said.

"They didn't think so." She shot him a look, surprised to see him staring at her as if he'd never seen her before.

Chapter Eight

Tucker wanted to scream at someone or at the least go outside and kick the side of the barn. No one had come to visit in two days. Addison had brought his meals and stayed to eat with him both days, but he was ready for Briar, Ford or even Julius. He looked at the 1918 calendar hanging in the hallway beside the bathroom door. Three weeks and Addison would remove the cast. He had marked the day with a big X.

"Doldrums?" She asked when she opened the bathroom door out into the landing. She carried a bucket with a wet rag draped over the side and the smell of soap followed her. Her hair looked like she'd stood on her head for a while before lightning shocked her. Wet spots on her overall knees attested to the fact she'd been scrubbing the floor.

"Not doldrums. Anger. Having to battle anger. I'm sick of being in the house. If I sit down in a straight back chair, could Briar and Ford carry me out on the porch?"

"You can go outside any time you can maneuver the stairs on your own. No reason you couldn't sit on the porch other than you'll freeze your ears off. Which reminds me, you need a haircut. I'll work that in tomorrow after I get the ironing done. I'm finished and lunch is sandwiches and soup. Olivia brought a quart yesterday. Want me to keep you company a while? I haven't read the paper yet today. Have you?"

"No. How bout we sit in a different room? That might help."

She set the bucket down and led the way into her bedroom. "Fine with me. Come on over into my room. Have a seat in the rocking chair and I'll fetch the newspaper. We can read it together."

He obeyed then got furious with himself. Three weeks ago he wouldn't have just sat where she told him; not without a fight. It was as if he had accepted her as a doctor and he just plain wasn't going to do that. Not now, not ever.

She sat cross-legged beside him and opened out the paper on the floor. "So it looks like sixteen men were drafted this week. Got a list of their names right here and their ages. Ruford Amos Henderson, Cletus Philip Matterhorn . . ."

"Go on. I don't need to hear all their names."

"Why haven't you been called up?"

"Don't know. I registered like everyone else. Just haven't got the call. Probably won't now with this leg, will I?"

"All these boys are eighteen or nineteen. You have a bad leg and you're old," she teased.

"Thirty is not old!"

"Depends on whether you are thirty or nineteen. How old was thirty when you were nineteen?"

"Ancient!" Tucker exclaimed.

She pointed to the paper. "Hey, look here. There's an article on that lady who's advocating birth control. They've put her in jail again."

"Skip it." Tucker could feel heat crawling up his neck and his cheeks.

"Does that topic embarrass you?"

"It's not something men and women discuss together," he said stoically.

"Not even husbands and wives?"

"We're not husband and wife so that ends the conversation."

"So you think birth control is wrong? Are you one of those who supported Anthony Comstock in his Comstock Law? Of course not, you weren't even born then, but I bet your old grandpa supported him. Do you realize what kind of problems that crazy law caused? Thank goodness some people ignored it and went on developing the—"

"Good grief, Addison, stop it now. This is not an appropriate conversation."

"Why? It's just a means of birth control. Of course, it is used for other things too."

"That's another reason why women shouldn't be doctors. They shouldn't be discussing things like this with men."

"But men can discuss the same thing with women patients, can they? Clara can go to a man doctor and he can deliver her baby and nothing is thought about it. I can't even talk about birth control without sending you spiraling out of your mind. It doesn't make a bit of sense to me, Tucker Anderson."

"I hear a car. Maybe it's Briar. I didn't say a woman couldn't deliver a baby did I? Midwives have been taking care of that for years and years. Nothing wrong with it. But there's a place for women and men. Women don't belong in the medical field except as nurses."

She folded her arms across her chest and glared at him. "We can give men baths and change their bedpans but we can't treat them?"

The hard knock on the door brought her to her feet. It couldn't be family because if the door was open, they came right inside. "This conversation is not over, Tucker. We'll finish it another day."

"Far as I'm concerned I don't ever want to hear anything about it again."

"Well, you will," she threw over her shoulder as she left.

She opened the living room door to find a tall, lanky man with his hat in his hand.

"You the doctor they're talkin' about in town? The one Magnolia wouldn't have?"

"I'm Dr. Carter," she said.

"You don't look like a doctor. You look like somebody's kid sister," he said.

"Why are you here?"

"It's my wife. She's in the car. Tryin' to birth a baby. Done fine with just me and her with the first three but she's been tryin' all night with this one and something ain't right. Heard you cured Granny Roberts and have been takin' care of Tucker. Can you just look at her?"

Addison opened the door. "Bring her inside. Can she walk up the stairs?"

"No, but I'll carry her. She's just a little thing even though she's about to birth a baby." He jumped off the porch and opened the door of the car. Three little boys, all under the age of six, piled out before he reached in and lifted a woman out.

"You boys get on in here out of the cold," Addison called out. "You and your father can keep Tucker company while we take care of this. Follow me," she led the way. By the time the man reached the spare bedroom right beside Tucker's, she had the bedding stripped and laying on the floor. A quick trip to her room and the bed was covered with a rubber sheet.

"Lay her here and shut the door behind you. Go talk to Tucker and don't come back unless I call you."

"Yes, ma'am," the man said.

Addison began removing the woman's shoes and stockings. Lord only knew why people thought they had to dress up to go to the doctor. "Hello, what's your name?"

The woman grabbed her swollen stomach and moaned. "I am Mary Sue. It won't come and it won't quit. There's something wrong in there. Even James wasn't this hard and he was my first born."

"Okay, Mary Sue, I'm going to take all these clothes off and drape a sheet over you so you won't feel naked."

"Water broke last night about the time we went to bed. Figured it'd be over by midnight," Mary said.

"Now that we've got you undressed and under the sheet, I want you to draw your knees up. I'm going to examine you. Do you understand what that means?"

She nodded, shut her eyes and turned her head to one side.

"It's breach and you're ready to deliver. There's going to be a lot of pressure but I'm going to attempt to turn this child. Take a deep breathe and let it out real slow. You'll be feeling my hand and there we go. Easy now, head down, preferably face down, too, but we'll take it face up." She talked to the baby. "There, we did it. Let's get ready to push, Mary."

"I been pushin' until I'm bone tired."

"This will produce results now. Contraction is coming. Push, push, push. Now relax. Next time don't hold your breath. Ever seen a puppy panting after he's been running around the yard?"

"Of course I have. What's that got to do with—oh, oh, oh," Mary Sue moaned.

"Pant like that puppy. That's the way. I can see a bit of black hair so it's coming now. Push again. Remember to pant in between. Here's a head."

"Is it alive?" Mary Sue asked.

A small whimper answered her question.

"Shoulder's. A big hind end that was clogging up the works. Fat rolls on her legs like she is already six months old. Big baby girl, Mary Sue." Addison cleaned out the baby's mouth and didn't even have to jiggle her for the crying to start.

"Can I see her?" Mary Sue reached.

"Let me take care of this umbilical cord and you can hold her. Once the placenta has passed, I'll give her a bath and get this bed cleaned up. You can stay here tonight," Addison said.

"I can't afford to stay all night. Just get things done and Wally can take me home."

Addison finished her job and stuck her head out the door to find Tucker leaning against the far wall, crutches under his arms. Wally was pacing the floor. Three little wide-eyed boys were huddled together near the bathroom door.

"It's a girl. Alive and healthy, just trying to come out

rear end first. I'm going to clean Mary Sue up and make her comfortable before you come in to see her. Give us twenty minutes."

Mary Sue crooned at the baby the whole time Addison went for a basin of water. "Ain't she beautiful? Guess I forgot to even bring a gown. We was just so afraid we'd lose the baby, we left so fast. Help me get back into my dress. It'll do until I get home."

"You're about the same size as I am. You can use one of mine. Now be very still while I get this sheet out from under you and a belly binder on you. We'll tighten it up every couple of hours all day long. In a couple of days you can stop using it but right now it supports your back and all that loose skin on your stomach."

In less than half an hour she had Mary Sue dressed, the bed changed, the baby bathed and wrapped in a clean sheet and ready for visitors. She opened the door to a still somber looking bunch of men and boys. "Hey, it's all right. Come right in and see the new baby."

The little boys hung back until they saw their mother all propped up and holding a mewling little baby. Then they rushed in to peek at their new sister. Wally kissed Mary Sue on the cheek and relief visibly washed over him. Tucker stayed in the doorway. He surely hoped Addison wasn't going to tell him every single detail of the birth but he wouldn't put it past her one bit.

"Wally, you can come back and visit about two this afternoon, if you want to," Addison said. "Tomorrow morning, you can take her home, but only if you promise me Mary Sue will have help for two weeks."

"I'm obliged to you Doc, I am. But we can't afford this kind of thing. I'll be hard put to pay you for what you already did. I'll just take them on home. I'm going to get Mary's momma over in Wilson and she'll be with us a month to help out."

"Where do you live?" Addison asked.

"About two miles on the other side of Healdton. Got a little farm. Twenty acres and I been doing some oilfield work in the day to keep a dollar coming in," Wally said.

"Got any hogs?" Addison asked.

"Few. Butchered four last month. What's that got to do with this baby and what I owe you?"

"We're out of bacon. I expect one good sized slab would pay the bill for what I've done and for Mary Sue to stay the day and night. I want to keep a close eye on her. Make sure there's no internal damage."

"Sounds fair enough to me," Wally said. "Boys, give your Momma a kiss and we'll drive down to Wilson and get Grandma. All right if we bring her back this afternoon during visitin' time?"

"That would be fine. And you might bring some diapers and a few little gowns for your new daughter," Addison suggested.

Mary Sue beamed. Wally kissed her again and shooed the boys out. Addison followed them and shut the door so the mother and father could have a few minutes of privacy with their newest child.

"I'm beholden to you," Mary Sue said when they were alone again. "I know a slab of bacon won't cover what all you've done but I thank you."

Addison picked up the hair brush from the vanity. "Here, let me comb your hair and braid it for you. And Mary Sue, you are very welcome. This isn't a real hospital but we'll do the best we can."

At noon Addison brought Tucker's tray to find him in a royal snit. One look at his face and there was no denying he was even more angry than he'd been early that morning. He didn't acknowledge her presence, just kept staring out the window at the bleak, gray sky.

"Soup and sandwiches," she said. "Chocolate cake with whipped cream for dessert."

"What are you serving the patient?" He said acidly.

"You are the patient."

"The other one. The one you brought in here without even asking me if it was all right. Clara and Tilly are paying you to take care of me."

Addison narrowed her eyes. "Six hundred dollars for forty-two days. That should be about fifteen dollars each day. Dock my pay for the twenty-four hours Mary Sue is here. That was a difficult birth and I will be sure there's no infection setting up before I let her go home. Now if you've got a problem with that Mr. Anderson, then I'll kick her out and take time to go check on her a couple of times today and tomorrow. I'd be a helluva a horrid doctor to send that woman back home right now."

"She can stay, but I'm not running a hospital out of

my house, Addison." He picked up the spoon and began to eat.

"I won't turn away anyone who's sick or needing my help. If you don't like that then I'll leave and forfeit my whole paycheck. I took an oath to help people. You're the big strong man who could run Evening Star with a broken leg, a cut hand and a mean attitude."

"Better go get her some food if she's going to be able to leave tomorrow like you told Wally. Can't have her starving and Wally shooting me for it," Tucker said with as much emotion as he would if he were discussing what color to paint the yard fence. She was right. He was wrong. He knew it. He'd never admit it.

Addison threw up her hands in a gesture of pure bewilderment. That man sure knew how to start an argument and not finish it. She'd like to push him down the steps that terrified him so badly. Oh, he thought he was being so secretive but she knew why he hadn't tried to get off the second floor. He'd developed a fear of falling which was totally natural after what had happened.

Mary Sue slept after lunch. Her family arrived promptly at two o'clock and left an hour later. They brought along baby clothing and diapers. Her mother even tucked in a pillow case to store the dirty laundry, saying they'd pick it up tomorrow morning.

Addison served supper, did the evening farm chores, avoided Tucker's room, not even wanting to fight with him over the birth control issue. She played with the new baby in the evening, told Mary Sue to ring the little bell she put on her bedside table if she needed her in the night and went to bed.

The next morning, Wally arrived at exactly ten o'clock to take the rest of his family home. He was so gentle and careful with Mary Sue that Addison had no doubt she'd be taken care of very well. There'd been no fever, no complaints of severe abdominal pain, and nothing that would indicate internal damage. The chubby little girl had simply gotten stuck.

They'd no more than cleared the driveway when another car came roaring down the lane. Addison stopped on the porch and looked to see if the sun was reflecting off the metal plate on the front of Tilly's vehicle. No, it was a pickup.

Must be Briar or Ford. They made sure they didn't have to listen to a crying baby before they came around.

"You the doctor we been hearing about?" A man yelled as he jumped from the truck.

"I guess I am," she said.

"My boy was chopping firewood and came nigh to cuttin' his thumb off. Can you fix it?"

"Bring him inside. I'll get my bag. Take him to the kitchen table." She took the stairs two at a time.

"What's Luke doing here?" Tucker called out from his room.

"Kid nearly amputated his thumb. Guess you'll have to dock me some more money." She slid down the banister like a child, bag in front of her.

"What's your name, son?" She asked as she took away the blood soaked towel from his hand.

"Hank," the boy whispered.

"How old are you?"

"Eleven."

"Then you are a big boy and you'll lie there and be still. Look the other way while I take a look at what we're dealing with."

"Can you fix it?" The father asked, his own voice strained as he looked at the deep laceration.

"Yes, and I need your help. I want you to draw me up some water in that basin. I'm going to put a shot of medicine straight into the cut and it's going to hurt bad, Luke. Then I'm going to clean it up and stitch it. There's bone showing but I can't see any chips out of the bone. It'll be a while before you can do any wood chopping again. You left-handed, Hank?"

He shook his head, his face pale with pain and fear.

She handed him the nearest dish cloth she could reach. "Then at least your dad won't have to feed you. Take a real deep breath and bite on this. Get ready. Now bite."

She injected the deadening medicine right into the cut. His eyes widened. His breath came in short gasps. But he bit down hard and didn't make a sound.

"Worst is over. Give it one minute and we'll put some more in but you won't feel anything else. You can spit that towel out and rest now. Your job is done."

"Will that put him to sleep?" Luke asked.

"No. It's a new drug they've developed for dentistry. Numbs the mouth so they can pull a tooth. I found it works the same with a cut. Here comes some more. Feel anything, Hank?"

He shook his head.

She pulled the two inch gaping gash together and began the tedious job of stitching skin back together. "When we get this done, I'm going to give you a tetanus shot. It'll feel like a bee sting and it'll be sore for a couple of days. I'll put it in your injured arm. That way both arms won't be sore. You've done very well so far so I expect you can handle that, too, can't you?"

"Yes, ma'am." Hank's bravado was returning.

"Good. We're ready to bandage this. I want to see you again tomorrow to change the dressing and then every other day for ten days. We'll take the stitches out then."

"You think he'll lose the use of that thumb?" Luke asked.

"At his age? I imagine by summer he'll be playing baseball and the scar will just be a white line. Here comes that shot."

"Ouch," he whined.

Luke grinned for the first time. "Just like a kid. Bite the bullet over a camel and yelp at a gnat."

"That's the way of it," Addison said.

"Reckon it'd be all right if we went up and checked on Tucker while we're here? We heard his hand got cut pretty bad, too, well as his leg bein' broke."

"He'd love the company, I'm sure. You tell him

you've got eleven stitches, Hank, and you were wide awake when you got them. Don't forget, day after tomorrow, I want to see you. And if red streaks start appearing from the bandage or if he gets feverish you bring him back immediately."

"Doc, about the bill?"

"How about you taking an hour every time you come just to sit and talk with Tucker? That'd free me up for a little while and be well worth the price," she said.

"Sounds like charity to me and I don't take charity," Luke said.

"Sounds like I might owe you. Five days. Five hours at least. With that old bear? Come on, how much more do I owe you?" She propped her hands on her hips and met his gaze across the table.

"It's a deal." Luke stuck out his hand and they shook over the top of a boy with a bandaged hand.

At lunch she took a tray up to Tucker's room to find him propped up in his bed, book in hand. He ignored her when she set the tray across his legs and figured she'd left the room by the time he laid the book aside and focused on a plate of roast beef slices setting on top of a thick slab of home made bread and topped with brown gravy. The woman could cook, that was a fact.

"Looks like a haircut is the next thing on the agenda." She said from the rocking chair. "What are you reading?"

He fought back a sigh. Drat the woman anyway. He didn't want to fight with her anymore today and that's what would happen if they talked. He was so tired of everyone singing her praises, he could scream. Luke and Hank both thought she could walk on water. He was glad they'd be coming around every couple of days. He could sure use the new faces but he didn't want his house thrown open to every one who got hurt for the next three weeks, either. To tell her so just brought on the debate.

"I'm reading Tom Sawyer again," he told her.

"Again?"

"Yes, again. I've read it a dozen times but it makes me laugh," he said.

"Well, bless my soul. I didn't know anything could make you laugh."

"That's because you don't know me."

"You eat and I'll get a towel and scissors." She decided to stop the fight right there. He could have the last word if he wanted.

He finished his lunch and without a word, got out of bed, and sat down in the chair in front of the vanity. He'd let her cut his hair to avoid the fight, but he was going to watch every move. After their fights, he wouldn't put it past her to shave his head. He sat as still as a statue while she draped a towel around his neck and began cutting his thick black hair. A woman hadn't touched his hair since he was a small boy and his mother had cut it once a month. After she died, he'd always gone into town to the barber. She ran her fingers through his hair and his pulse raced. His scalp tingled.

His heart skipped a beat. He definitely needed to get off this floor and go outside. Nothing was right in his world anymore.

She cut a while then stood in front of him, cocking her head to one side and making sure everything was even. She placed her palms on his cheeks and turned his face this way and that.

Her hands were like fire on his skin. He looked past her in the vanity mirror, amazed that there weren't red streaks on his face. Then he looked into her eyes, not six inches from his—green, bottomless, and staring into his own eyes. As if she were looking so deep into his soul she could see everything he'd ever done or would do in his lifetime.

Before he could blink, she leaned forward, shut those stunning green eyes and kissed him. Full out kissed him. Right on the mouth. Setting every nerve in his body to quivering.

He reached up with his left hand and tangled his fingers in her curly hair, holding her lips tighter to his as he kissed her back. When she broke away, he wanted more.

"Wow."

"Why'd you do that?" He asked.

"Because I wondered what an old bear would kiss like. Very nice, I might say," she smiled.

His heart did an unfamiliar dance in his chest. "Don't do it again."

"You liked it, Tucker Anderson. Of course, it broke

my training. I'm not supposed to get involved with the patient. Rest assured, it won't happen again. It was nice. Very nice. Now I know and I'm not one to go against the rules more than once."

Chapter Nine

Sleep was more elusive than chasing a fairy through a rainforest. Flat on his back, Tucker couldn't get comfortable. He blamed it on the cast which kept him from rolling onto his left side. He sighed. He tried shutting his eyes and counting sheep but that didn't work. He counted baby calves cavorting in a pasture. Nothing worked. Feeling as if his whole body and soul were encased in a cast instead of only his leg, he finally arose to keep from smothering under the weight of it all. Using only the furniture to brace himself, he hobbled to the rocking chair and drew back the curtains. Stars scattered like diamonds on a lady's blue velvet dancing dress glittered in the dark sky. A big, round, full moon hung there amongst them—a god among millions of worshipers. He touched the window pane. Cold, even on the inside, but the embers in the fireplace barely glowed.

Something tickled his arm and he brushed away a common house fly. One who'd survived the bitter northers by hiding in a corner of his house. Didn't the idiot know he still had a fly swatter? Looking around on his pajama bottoms and shirt for the insect, he suddenly realized the problem. It was the pajamas. He'd been in them more than three weeks now and they were the thing keeping him down. Until he put on his overalls and flannel shirt, he'd never be able to conquer those stairs. In the night clothes, he was an invalid dependent upon others. To be a man, he needed to dress like one.

Addison had said he could go outside whenever he could get there on his own volition. She didn't say it had to be daylight when he did it. He couldn't sleep. He wanted to be anywhere but confined on the second floor of his house. Just thinking about breaking the restraining, invisible chains was enough for him to unbutton the pajama top and pick up his crutches. He almost gave up the idea when he pulled on long handles. They stretched over the cast with no problem, but by the time he fastened the final button, he was exhausted.

"See what laziness causes. If they'd let me get up and work from the first day, I wouldn't be in this condition," he grumbled under his breath.

The flannel shirt wasn't a problem at all, but the overalls refused to fit over the cast and the underwear.

That didn't deter him one bit. Using his pocket knife, he carefully ripped the inside seam. That could be repaired easily enough when his leg healed. The outside one had been felt seamed and if he'd cut the fabric there, the overalls would be ruined. Getting a sock and shoe on his right foot was no easy task, but he triumphed even if it did take him ten minutes.

He was a man again. At least that's what he told the shadow in the mirror above the vanity. One thing for sure, he was taking charge of his life and tomorrow he was going to the barn to help feed. He might not be able to drive yet, but if he leaned on the back of the truck, he could toss hay over the fence.

Quietly, he made his way out into the dark hallway. Addison's door was shut so she wouldn't know what he was up to. She'd be surprised tomorrow morning to find him in the living room or the kitchen. He reached the top of the steps and looked down. He couldn't do it. Absolutely could not. It had to be a mile to the bottom. What if he fell? What if he rolled and landed at the bottom with a broken neck. He'd never see Clara's baby. Tonight wasn't the night after all. He'd go back to his room and keep his clothing on until morning. From now on, he'd be dressed every day. Maybe that step was enough for one night.

He leaned against the wall and suddenly the warmth of Addison's lips on his was very real. Expecting to see her in front of him, a taunting bossy look on her face, he snapped his eyes open. She wasn't there but her kiss had come back to haunt him. What woman kissed a man? It was supposed to be the other way around. Men initiated the kissing. Women didn't?

Not unless they are in charge because you are a panty waist.

So that's why she'd kissed him. He was an invalid who couldn't even master a simple flight of stairs. Not that he didn't enjoy the kiss; he couldn't remember the last time a kiss had stirred his senses into a jumble of raw desire. It would never happen again, she'd said. She wouldn't break the rules a second time. That didn't mean he couldn't. If he decided he wanted to kiss her, then he'd do it. It wouldn't just be very nice either. It would be damn wonderful.

He looked down into the black abyss and shut his eyes. One step at a time was all he had to do. If he took the first one and couldn't go any further, he could go back. He slid one crutch down the stairs. It hit the bottom with a thud and he hoped the noise didn't wake Addison. Surely it wouldn't. She'd had a very busy day: chores in the morning, bringing both his and Mary Sue's breakfast, whatever she did all morning in the way of housekeeping, lunch, Mary Sue going home, Hank needing stitches, supper, evening chores. The woman must be exhausted every evening.

Positioning the left crutch under his arm and gripping the banister with his right hand until his knuckles were white, he carefully took the first step to freedom.

Fifteen times he panicked, dried his clammy right hand, remembered to breathe so he wouldn't pass out, set his mind on fresh air. Finally, he reached the bottom and retrieved the second crutch. He crossed the foyer, went through the dining room and into the kitchen. Forget the front porch. He was going out to the barn to see Bill and the calf Addison hand saved.

Addison had been kissed before but nothing had shaken her all the way to the bottom of her roots. Even after she turned out the light and went to bed, she kept touching her lips to see if they were really on fire. She couldn't sleep but she couldn't turn on the light. Tucker would know for sure he had affected her if he saw the light under the door or heard her rumbling around. She was careful to lie very still so the metal bedsprings wouldn't give away her restlessness. At least until she heard Tucker's squeaking bed pronounce that he was having just as much trouble sleeping.

She didn't even have to strain her hearing powers to know when Tucker crawled out of bed to sit in his chair. He muttered and she knew the tone even if she didn't understand the words. There was enough thumping around across the hall that if there'd been dead people in the house, he would have woken them up. For a long time she couldn't figure out what he was doing, then she heard the familiar squeak of the wardrobe door. The man was getting dressed. That meant he had intentions of going outside in the middle of the night.

Addison smiled in the darkness and listened closer. The kiss had prompted him to face his fears. Most likely so that he could dismiss her early. Men didn't like women to kiss them. Not that they didn't enjoy kissing. Lord only knew how much they liked that, and He was the only one who knew. However, it sure messed with their manhood to have a woman kiss them first, even if they enjoyed it. Just like women being doctors—it wasn't acceptable in society. And again, Lord only knew why society had so much power.

When he stopped at the top of the steps, she held her breath until her sides ached. He'd be worse than an old bear if he didn't succeed in his mission. She said a prayer and hoped it didn't stall out at ceiling level.

God, please help this man face his fears. Give him the strength, both natural and mental to fight the battle and be a winner. Amen.

She eased out of bed, threw a shawl around her shoulders and opened the door enough to peek out. The only light in the hallway was what little the moon cast through the curtains in the bedrooms, but she could see a large dark form near the stairs, leaning against the wall. She slid down onto the floor and continued her vigil. How long did he intend to fight the demons? An hour? Two? Would he go back to bed and not whip the fear?

A crutch slid down the stairs and landed at the bottom with a definite thud on the wooden floor. He took the first step and gasped. It wasn't easy to sit still. Her first impulse was to rush out and help him, but to regain his confidence and pride, he needed to do this on his own. He'd make it. He had to since he'd thrown a crutch down the stairs. How else would he explain it to her, come morning?

Positioning the left crutch under his arm and gripping the banister with his right hand until his knuckles were white, he carefully took the first step to freedom. Fifteen times he panicked, dried his clammy right hand, remembered to breathe so he wouldn't pass out, set his mind on fresh air. Finally, he reached the bottom and retrieved the second crutch. He crossed the foyer, went through the dining room and into the kitchen. Forget the front porch. He was going out to the barn to see Bill and the calf Addison had saved.

Addison had been kissed before but nothing had shaken her all the way to the bottom of her roots. Even after she turned out the light and went to bed, she kept touching her lips to see if they were really on fire. She couldn't sleep, but she couldn't turn on the light. Tucker would know for sure he had affected her if he saw the light under the door or heard her rumbling around. She was careful to lie very still so the metal bedsprings wouldn't give away her restlessness. At least until she heard Tucker's squeaking bed pronounce that he was having just as much trouble sleeping.

She didn't even have to strain her hearing to know when Tucker had crawled out of bed to sit in his chair.

He muttered and she knew the tone even if she didn't understand the words. There was enough thumping around across the hall that if there'd been dead people in the house, he would have wakened them. For a long time she couldn't figure out what he was doing, then she heard the familiar squeak of the wardrobe door. The man was getting dressed. That meant he had intentions of going outside in the middle of the night.

When she realized where he was going, she wanted to join him. To tell him about the calf and how it had grown so much in the past few days. How that Bill guarded it day and night, leaving the barn only for minutes each day. Share with him the news of how his farm had been well-cared for in his absence. Common sense told her to stay in her room and let him discover all those things for himself. It was his and he'd made it clear he didn't want to share anything with her from the beginning.

She watched through the window as he expertly crossed the yard. He'd learned how to make those crutches do the work for him and her heart swelled with joy. A dim light came on in the barn and Bill yelped. Reunion time.

Bill greeted Tucker with a yelp and a tail that refused to stop wagging. Tucker responded by bending at the waist and scratching the dog's ears. "So you been keeping things together like a good friend?"

Bill just wagged his tail harder and ran back to the

stall where his ward lay sleeping in a far corner. Tucker followed. "Smells like perfume in here. Didn't know how much I missed the smell of cow manure. Hey look at this, Bill. This what you forsook me for? Well, it's a prime example of a winter calf born too early. Would've frozen to death if you and Addison hadn't found it. Course you're the one who's kept it safe from coyotes and the like. I'm proud of you, boy."

He checked the tack room. Nothing out of place. Hay forks even hung on the nails where they belonged. Evidently Addison was neat in her outside work too. He shivered and remembered he'd been in such a hurry to escape the confines of the house, he hadn't even put on a coat. That limited the amount of time he could spend in the barn for sure.

"Gotta go, Bill. But I'll be back in the morning." He extinguished the lantern he'd lit when he first walked into the barn.

Addison saw the light go out and realized when he started back toward the house he wasn't wearing a jacket. So the first outing had been cut short by the cold. At least he'd proven himself. She listened intently. The back door opened and closed. The racket of him crossing the hardwood floor in the dining room echoed through the house. It stopped in the living room and she swore she heard a sigh as he lowered himself onto the settee. She returned to bed and pulled the covers up to her chin. Even after several hours she could feel the heat between them when she kissed him and that's what she dreamed of when she drifted off into a deep sleep.

She awoke to the mixed aromas of bacon and coffee creeping under her door. Addison was out of bed in an instant, pulling her overalls on as she made her way to the kitchen. She'd had a bad night but she'd never over-slept before, not even one time in medical school. When she hurried through the door she found Tucker sitting at the table, fully dressed, his leg with a cast sup-ported on a chair. *Tom Sawyer* was propped in front of his plate which was piled high with bacon, toast and scrambled eggs.

He didn't look up or offer any explanations. "Food's in the warmer. Help yourself."

She poured a cup of coffee and joined him at the table. "So you ready to help with the morning chores?"

He almost dropped his fork but retrieved it before it hit the floor. "You getting tired of doing them? It's part of the job you took on from what Briar tells me."

"It is, but if you want to help I'd be obliged." She sipped the hot, black coffee, made exactly to her liking.

"You're not going to fight me on it. I figured you'd have a fit and try to send me back to bed. I had a whole speech ready."

"Surprise! I think it would do you good to get fresh air. If you get too tired, I can always bring you back to the house. Chores don't have to be completed before daylight."

"If you're going to heaven they do." He looked down at his book but couldn't focus. Dammit! He didn't want her to give him the go-ahead to stay out of bed, to travel up and down the steps, to help do his own chores. He'd looked forward to the debate all night.

"You figurin' on eating breakfast before we go?"

"Sure am. Not often a man cooks for me. I wouldn't waste that for anything." She got up and went toward the stove.

"I didn't cook for you. I cooked for myself and there was too much."

"Doesn't matter what you say, I'm going to tell Clara and Tilly that you cooked for me. Mmmm." She sniffed inside the warmer.

"Don't you dare be telling things like that. People will talk and I don't like it."

"So what? Have you always liked everything that happened in your life? Did you like being confined to the second floor? Did you like having measles or chicken pox? Quite frankly, Tucker, I don't care what you like. I don't care if you like or dislike women doctors. I don't care if it offends your masculinity to have it talked about that you cooked for the doctor who's living with you—"

"Whoa, stop right there." He held up his hand. "You are hired help, not someone who's living with me. Holy hell, Addison, your reputation would be shot and I'd be expected to make an honest woman of you and it'll be a cold day in hell before that happens. So don't you go around saying such things."

"Don't you shush me when I'm talking. I'm not a child and you won't treat me like one. I'm a doctor and I would appreciate you acting like I am."

"You might think you are, but honey, it takes more than an education to be a doctor."

"Oh, and what does it take? Being a male? You should have been born in the days of the cave men. That way you could go out and drag a woman home by the hair to cook and clean your cave for you."

"Sounds like a good deal to me."

"You are ruining my breakfast. Eat and hush."

"Don't tell me to eat and hush. I'm not a child either."

"Okay, then," she said, exasperation in her voice. "Let's start all over. Good morning, Tucker. It's good to see you feeling well enough to get dressed and come down for breakfast. My, that smells good. Are there any leftovers? I'd sure enjoy some before I go out and do the chores."

"Why, yes, I made a plate for you and stuck it in the warmer," he growled, thinking the game she was playing was even more childish than the fight, but playing along so she wouldn't have the last word.

"Thank you." She set about eating and didn't look at him. She'd provoked the fight because she was still angry about his reaction to the kiss. Going all masculine like he had to prove to the world he still carried a club and wore animal skins. Breakfast was filling but she didn't taste a bite of it. She ate everything on her plate, took it to the sink, and went to the back door where her work boots stood waiting.

"So are we ready?" He pushed his plate back, leaving it on the table for her to take care of later.

"I am. Are you?"

He didn't bother to answer but grabbed his crutches.

She didn't wait to help him get into his heavy winter coat but plowed right outside, leaving the door open for the cold wind to whistle through. If he was so ready to take care of himself, he could just figure out a way to stand on one leg, get a coat on and not drop his crutches. That man could aggravate a pure saint and no one had ever accused Addison Carter of having wings and a halo. At least no one outside of Carter County and they sure didn't know her around here.

He leaned his right crutch on the wall beside the door and very slowly and carefully managed to get his coat on and buttoned up all the way. He was feeling right smug when he reached for the crutch and it fell flat on the floor. He bent at the waist as far as he could, but couldn't reach the thing.

"Dammit!" he swore loudly, but refused to call out to Addison to come back inside to help him. Granted, she was overpaid, but he wouldn't have her gloating about still being needed. Matter of fact, if she didn't straighten up her attitude he just might fire her on the spot. He could take care of himself.

Using the walls and cabinets for support, he hopped to the table where he pushed a chair back across the floor. Too bad if it left marks on her freshly waxed floor.

"Dammit," he swore again. It wasn't her floor. It was his and if he wanted to spill paint in the middle of it and smear it around with a kitchen towel, he'd do so.

By the time he positioned the chair just right to sit down, then lean to one side and pick up the crutch, she was parked beside the back porch and honking the truck horn. With his head held high, he made his way to the driver's side and opened the door. "Slide over. I'm driving."

"How? You can't clutch with a cast."

He hadn't thought about that. His jaw muscles worked double-time. He slammed the door and went around the truck to the passenger's side. Even then he needed Addison's helping hand to drag him inside. It wouldn't be long before he had the cast off and then he'd stand on both his legs and gladly wave goodbye to the spitfire.

Chapter Ten

Hard rain mixed with sleet battered at the windows and sounded like rocks hitting the roof. Addison drew her shawl tighter and her chair another foot closer to the fireplace. In two more weeks her job would be finished at Evening Star. She'd been there a mouth and Tucker had proven Tilly to be a pure prophet. He'd been grouchy, self-willed, demanding—everything Tilly had declared that first day when Addison had taken the job. However, the experience had been good and the pay at the end of the job would make it all worthwhile.

"You want this newspaper?" Tucker asked from his overstuffed chair. Already there were thirteen piled up beside the arm.

"Yes, I do, and tomorrow if it's not raining, I'm burning that stack." She reached across to take the paper from his hands.

"It's not up to the top yet," he argued, just like he did with everything she said or did. "When it gets to the top then I'll burn it."

"No, you won't, you'll move it to the bedroom or the dining room and before long this place will look like a rat's nest again. Which reminds me, I had to set mouse traps when I cleaned the place out. Those *will be* taken care of by the end of the week, Tucker. If you don't burn them, I will. Don't you have any pride? Evening Star is a beautiful ranch. Any woman would be glad to hang her hat by the back door and call this home."

Tucker grunted.

"Don't you make that noise at me."

"Don't you preach at me. You went to school to be some high-powered doctor, not a preacher. If I want a sermon, I'll call Julius. Besides, you're just a drifter, Addison Carter. You drifted into town to show all the male doctors you could work for a big, important oil company and you'll drift out in two weeks. Drifters don't give permanent residents advice and they don't berate the way they keep their property."

"You have as much sensitivity as a full-grown boar hog. No wonder you're not married."

"Don't you start on that. Have you seen one thing

wrong with this farm? It's clean as a whistle. My live-stock are fat and sassy even in the cold winter. Even my dog, Bill, is well-fed and loves me."

"I'm not talking about your farm. It's perfect. I love Evening Star. I could live here forever now that the house looks like people and not animals live here. It's you, Tucker. Everyone in the whole town thinks you are some kind of model citizen. Even Julius and Olivia praise your fine Christian ways. Either you've got everyone in Healdton fooled or else you just plain hate me because I'm a doctor."

"I haven't ever tried to fool anyone. Guess it's be-cause you're a doctor."

"That kiss we shared didn't say you minded anything about me."

"That was a mistake."

They were interrupted by a loud knock on the door.

"I'm sick of people coming here at all hours of the night for you to doctor them. You're supposed to be in private practice," he grumbled.

"Okay, I'll just turn away whoever it is. Tell them to go bleed to death or bury their stillborn child tomorrow. I'll tell them you don't want to share my skills with the community since I'm in private practice."

The next knock was heavier, more urgent.

"It's your call. I'm waiting." She didn't get out of the chair.

"Oh, go on. I'll just be glad when the next two weeks are finished and my life can get back to normal."

A man yelled as she crossed the foyer and flung open the door. "Doc? Oh, I was afraid you weren't home. Can you look at my baby? She can't breathe and she's turning blue."

Addison left the door open and stepped back. "Get her in here."

The man motioned toward the car and a woman came running with a toddler in her arms, the cold rain soaking them. "I borrowed my neighbor's car over in Wirt. All I got is a wagon and . . ."

"Put the baby right here," Addison listened with one ear and cleared the dining room table at the same time. "What's her name?"

"Annabel." The mother shivered.

Addison's voice soothed as she listened to the baby's heart. "Hello, Annabel. You sound fine there, little girl. Now let's check your throat. Mommie, can you hold her little head so I can get a look to see if there's blockage?"

The mother held Annabel and Addison pried her mouth. The child sucked in a lung full of air and bellowed while she kicked and screamed against the stranger looking down her throat. Color came back to her mouth while she yelled. "That's good, honey. Let's check the nose while we've got you good and mad. Hold her head just a little longer." Annabel clamped her mouth shut and her lips turned blue again.

Addison ignored the whimpers and reached for a pair of long handled tweezers. "Uh-huh, there's the culprit. Has she been wheezing?"

"Ever since this morning. Like she can't get air. Sometimes she'd gasp real loud."

Addison pulled a dried bean from Annabel's nostril. "Here's the reason. She was barely getting any air past the bean and every so often she'd have to get air through her mouth. Now, let's take another look. Oops, looks like she's had a lot of fun." Addison pulled the second one out.

Annabel's screams got louder when Addison looked inside the other side of her nose. "It's all right sweetheart. I'd fuss too if someone was digging around in my nose. Here's our next culprit. Bet you cooked beans today, didn't you?"

"Yes, I did." The mother shivered again. "I spilled them on the floor. Guess I missed a few when I cleaned up the mess."

"There's only one in this side. It gave her a little space but not enough to keep a good airflow. I'm going to put some drops in her nose to keep it from infecting, and I think she'll be fine. Now, Mom, how about you? You're shivering and you could take a cold or pneumonia if you don't get out of those wet clothes."

"I'll be fine. I'm so grateful to you. I thought there we'd lose her for sure." The mother held the child close to her wet dress.

"Yes, you will be fine. You're going to go in the kitchen right there and shed all those wet clothes. There's extra things here you can wear home and an extra blanket you can wrap around Annabel. Be a shame to loose you both to pneumonia after we've saved Annabel."

"We don't take charity; we can pay the bill," the man said stiffly.

"Of course you will. I don't work for free. Do you work for Magnolia?"

"No, for Rose Oil."

"Then tomorrow you return the borrowed clothing and blankets to Briar. He's a cousin-in-law to Tucker Anderson who owns this house. Now about your bill?"

"I got money."

"Then it will be one dollar for the office visit. Do you want a receipt?"

He handed her a bill. "No, ma'am. Reckon we both know that you fixed Annabel and I paid. And we thank you for the use of the dry things for my wife and blanket for the baby."

"You are very welcome. I'll just be a moment getting them. Tucker is in the living room. You ever met him?"

"Once or twice when he's come to the wells to visit with Mr. Nelson."

"Then go on there and warm your hands by the fire. Would you like dry things?"

"I'll be fine. A warming by the fire will dry me out enough to get me home."

Addison opened the closet door in one of the spare rooms and found a faded day dress. Surely Tucker wouldn't pitch too big of a fit if she borrowed one of his mother's old things for the lady downstairs. A quick search in the bureau drawers produced a camisole and a pair of underpants. She had to open another drawer to find warm socks and a sweater. A coat with patches on the sleeves hung on the back of the door. She grabbed it and a blanket from the hall closet and literally ran to the kitchen.

She knocked on the door and waited. "It's me," she finally said.

"Come in," the lady answered.

Addison found her sitting in front of the cook stove which was still warm from supper. She hadn't taken off a single article of clothing but Annabel was naked and asleep.

"I'll put the things right here on the table and hold the baby while you change." Modesty wasn't anything new to her. She'd seen all kinds of people during her internship. Those who'd bare everything and those who had to be coerced into unfastening their shirt so she could listen to their heartbeat.

"Yes, ma'am. I didn't introduce myself. I'm Ida Jones. My husband is Matthew. We're grateful to you for taking care of Annabel." She handed the baby to Addison.

Addison wrapped her in a blanket, drew up a chair to the warm stove and enjoyed holding the baby. "I'm Dr. Addison Carter, and I'm glad to make your acquaintance. You don't sound like you're from this area?"

"From Virginia. Matthew worked for Mr. Nelson in Pennsylvania and we moved here to work. We've got a house in Wirt and in a few more months, Matthew says we're getting an automobile. It takes a long time to save up for one but he makes good wages. He's a supervisor," she said proudly.

"I see," Addison had the urge to hum lullabies. Annabel was a cherub. Fat little cheeks. Dark hair. Lashes lying on her cheeks and a perfect little rosebud mouth.

"I have to admit, it does feel good to get into dry things. I was so frightened with the baby when she turned blue that I didn't even take time to put on a coat. I'll be more careful next time I spill beans," Ida said.

"It's pretty common. Most of the time they just shove it up one side though and the parents think they're coming down with a cold. After the ordeal tonight, she'll probably never put anything else in there. By the same token, she won't let you or me near her to look inside her nose when she's sick, either."

"I can hold her down if a doctor needs to look inside her nose. I'm not sure I could get anything out without hurting her, so that's fine by me. Are you staying in Healdton? Would you be interested in setting up practice over in Wirt? If you hadn't been here, we'd a had to go all the way to Ardmore in this storm."

"No, I'm not staying in Healdton. I'm just drifting through for six weeks then I'm offering to go serve in the war."

"Too bad. I'm expecting another baby here in about six months. It'd be nice to have a woman doctor to look after things. I know the other women over in Wirt would like that, too."

"Thank you." Addison handed Annabel over to her mother.

"Think on it. Drifters have to come to roost some day."

Tucker was up early the next morning. The rain had stopped, thank goodness, or he'd be stuck inside the house all day. As it was, Addison might refuse to let him go help with chores. He could hear her condescending voice telling him that his crutches would sink into the mud and he'd fall.

He fired up the stove and crumbled a fistful of sausage into a cast iron skillet. He'd make biscuits and gravy, along with potatoes fried with onions. Bit by bit, he was taking over his household. He'd be glad when the cast was removed and he could stack newspapers all the way to the ceiling.

Not that he would. He liked the cleanliness, the brightness, all of it. It reminded him of the days before his mother died, when everything smelled good and the sunshine poured through sparkling clean windows.

He measured out a cup of flour, two teaspoons of baking powder and one of soda into a bowl. He cut in a half a cup of butter and added buttermilk until the mixture was just barely sticky. Next he shook a little flour on the cabinet top, kneaded the dough and cut the biscuits with the same glass his mother always used.

"Smells good in here," Addison said. "I could get

spoiled to having breakfast started when I rise, but this is really part of my job. You don't have to cook until I leave."

"By then I wouldn't be able to lift an egg."

She poured a cup of coffee and stirred the sausage as she sipped. When he had the biscuits in the pan, she slid it in the oven. "Potatoes?" She asked.

"I'll peel if you'll get the onions frying."

She chose a small black skillet and added bacon drippings from a can on the back of the stove. By the time the grease was hot, she had peeled a small onion, slicing it into thin rings. They sizzled when she tossed them in and added Tucker's potatoes.

He made gravy. She set the table. He stirred the potatoes. She poured coffee. She brought it to the table. He said grace. They ate in silence, each reading a section of the morning paper. She read about the cantina being built next to the railroad in Ardmore to accommodate the soldiers using the train to get home when their enlistments were finished. He read about the price of cattle feed and an article on how several farmers were already out of hay and having to pay high dollar for what little was for sale.

She laid her portion of the paper on the table, gathered up the dirty dishes and put them in the sink. "Ready to do chores? Looks like we've got sun. Can't see a cloud in the sky." She looked out the above the sink.

"Pretty muddy, ain't it?"

"You being lazy?"

"No, I just figured you'd say my crutches would sink in the mud." His temper flared. No one had ever accused Tucker Anderson of being lazy.

"They might. Tires on the truck could sink, too. I reckon we can take care of it. I'll pull the truck close as I can to the back door. I'll do the work but it'll do you good to get out."

He hobbled to the back door, grabbed his coat and hat and had them on before she finished washing the table. That woman would exasperate Jesus Christ, Himself.

Addison couldn't understand Tucker. One day he was so eager to go outside he was a pest; the next, he was inventing reasons to keep himself inside. The man would frustrate a saint.

She was able to get so close to the porch steps that he didn't have to put his crutches in the mud. He'd become quite adept at slinging them in the back of the truck, using the door to balance and sliding himself into the passenger side of the black truck. When she parked inside the barn, he hopped along on his good leg to the truck bed and grabbed the crutches. Using only one, he'd figured out a way to sling hay bales to her and she stacked them neatly.

"No baby calves, today," she said when they reached the pasture. "I was worried about that old girl over there." She pointed to a heifer, round with a calf. "Looks like she might have some trouble when her time comes. Probably have to pull the calf. It's her first one, isn't it?"

"Yes, it is. She's pretty small too. I don't think she'll calve before spring. She's just big. Might be twins."

"Could be," Addison agreed. "You stay inside. I'll throw it off to them."

"I'm getting out," he declared.

"If I told you not to jump over the side of a volcano, I do believe you'd do it just to show me you could."

He opened the door and reached for his crutches. "Probably. I don't like women telling me what to do."

"You surely have proved that point these past few weeks. Do you ever plan to marry and have a family?"

"Thought about it. Got the bug last fall when Clara and Briar married. They just seemed so happy. Then I watched Tilly and Ford. God, they were both so miserable, I figured they'd never admit they loved each other. I don't know if I will or not, but if and when I do, the woman won't tell me what to do."

"Where you going to get a woman like that?" Using the hay hooks she grabbed a bale and dragged it to the back of the truck.

He leaned on the truck until she got it within reach. It was his turn then. He clipped the baling wire and holding the bale together as best he could, wrapped his arms around it and tossed it over the barbed wire fence.

"Where am I going to get her? I'm not. If the Good Lord has a mind for me to be married, then I expect He'll drop the woman out of the sky and right in the middle of the Evening Star."

"Right!" She blew out a cloud of vapor into the bitter cold morning with every breath she exhaled. "That's really good thinking, Tucker. I think God has a lot more to worry over than your love life. If you're waiting on an angel to float down from heaven on a white, fluffy cloud, then you've got a big disappointment in store."

"We'll see. Clara got Briar and Tilly got Ford. They weren't looking and even though it wasn't what they really wanted, it's worked out wonderful."

"Then what makes you think God is going to give you what you really want. Maybe who He's going to send you is someone you can't stand at first, either."

"Someone like you?"

"Oh, no, honey, someone even worse. I'm leaving in less than two weeks. Someone who'll stay forever."

"Worse than you? Honey," he drawled the endearment sarcastically. "God doesn't know how to be that evil."

Chapter Eleven

What started out in a flurry of excitement in the local drug store ended six weeks later at five o'clock in a rather anticlimactic fashion. Addison's trunks were packed. Briar and Ford hauled them down to Tilly's car. Tilly handed her an envelope with eighteen one hundred dollar bills in it: twelve hundred from her and Clara for caring for Tucker, six hundred from Briar because he didn't have to take on morning and evening chores. Early that morning she'd removed Tucker's cast, declared the bone had mended well and gave him a series of exercises to rebuild the muscle in his leg. He'd been in the living room when she left and barely said goodbye.

Addison didn't look back. To do so would have brought on tears and she wouldn't cry. She'd miss

Evening Star. She'd worry about that heifer that looked like she would birth an elephant. She'd think about Bill standing guard over the little calf in the barn. Memories of all those papers burning would stay with her for years, and she'd wonder how long it would take Tucker to make the house just as messy as she'd found it. She'd fallen in love with the place but it was a one-sided affair.

"I sure wish you'd give up this idea of the war and stay in Healdton," Tilly said.

"And what? There're not many folks who can pay for private care like you did and those who can usually only want to hire a nurse, not a doctor. I can go home and face the sneers of all my friends and family or I can escape into the army."

"Well, before I take you over to Ardmore, Beulah wants us to stop by for supper. That all right?"

"Sounds lovely. I'd like to see her and Cornelia again so I can tell them goodbye. She's a sweet lady."

"Yes, been like a grandmother to me at times. She had this good friend, Bessie, who was even more out-spoken than Beulah. She passed away a few months ago. Beulah has sure missed her."

"It's not easy being the last one in a generation, but unless Beulah's heart plays out, she appears to be healthy." Addison felt the sting of having to enlist when it was the furthest thing from her true dream.

"Here we are." Tilly pulled her car in behind a whole string of others.

"What's going on?"

"Guess Beulah is receiving guests tonight or else there's a big run on those empty rooms she's got to let out," Tilly said.

Addison walked into a warm room with people everywhere. Julius and Olivia, Cornelia and George, Nellie, Briar and Clara, Ford and Tucker. She wondered how in the devil he'd beat her to Beulah's but before she could say a word, Beulah tapped a fork against a crystal water glass to get everyone's attention.

"Our guest of honor has arrived. Dulcie has dinner on the table so come and find your seats."

Addison looked around to see who she was talking about.

"It's you," Tilly whispered. "You are the guest of honor."

"Me?" Addison cocked her head to one side.

"That's right." Clara looped her arm through Addison's. "And you deserve to be after the six weeks you just endured."

"Here, here! If she deserves that honor, so do I, since I put up with her sass all those weeks too," Tucker said.

It hadn't been easy watching her walk out the door. He wanted to grab her hand and beg her to stay but a man couldn't ask a woman such a thing. If she hadn't been a doctor and it hadn't been a job, her reputation would have been in shreds already. Somehow the whole town had overlooked the fact that they'd lived together all those weeks without benefit of a chaperone in the house. Perhaps it was because a big majority of them had needed her services and thought she was some kind of demi-god. He'd been amazed when he realized he wasn't ready to see her leave, astonished to finally admit to himself that she was a damn fine doctor as well as farmer—not to mention a worthy adversary in a debate. They'd fought. They'd kissed that one time. He'd be alone again, and he didn't like that feeling one bit.

"You were an old bear more than ninety percent of the time," Clara told him.

"I made breakfast the last two weeks. Every morning," he said.

"Come on children. No fighting tonight. We're honoring Doctor Addison and we'll have no arguments. That goes for the rest of you, too." Beulah shook her finger at them.

Beulah offered grace when they'd all found their places and began passing bowls and platters. Fried chicken. Mashed potatoes. Steaming, hot yeast rolls. Green beans with bacon floating in them. Creamed corn. Sweet potatoes topped with brown sugar and pecans.

"This is a meal fit for a queen. Thank you for such a fine send-off," Addison said.

"Depends," Beulah said.

"What are you talking about?" Addison asked.

"First things first," Beulah said. "Nellie?"

"I've taken a job over in Tishomingo teaching high

school English. My sister lives there and we'll be staying together. I'm leaving tomorrow and I wanted to tell you all goodbye. I've loved staying all these years at the Morning Glory, but it's time for me to move on and be around my family."

"Oh, my," Clara said. "Have they hired a replacement?"

"Yes, I wouldn't go until they did. A fine lady who followed her husband here for the oil business. I was surprised they'd hire a married woman. It's not done very often but her credentials are wonderful. Goes to show that despite Tucker's feelings about married women working, times are changing."

"Don't get him on that soap box tonight," Tilly said. "If he gets started no one will be able to shut him up."

Tucker shook his head and shoveled in a fork full of corn. He'd never agree with women working outside the home. It wouldn't be the first time he and Nellie locked horns and both refused to budge.

"We'll miss you so much," Clara said.

"And I'll miss every one of you. Can't say I'm not looking forward to going though. My sister has a cute little two bedroom house and since her husband died, she's been begging me to come live with her. I'm really looking forward to it."

"Now Cornelia." Beulah looked down the table and the couple on the far end.

"George has asked me to marry him. I said yes so

there will actually be two new faces at the school here in Healdton. I'll be working full time in the drug store with him."

George grinned and took Cornelia's hand in his. "You'll be wondering about the divorce. My lawyer has taken care of it. Inez signed the papers and didn't contest anything. Because she deserted me for another man, it's final now, so we can marry soon. We aren't having a wedding as such. Simply going to the courthouse on Friday. We plan to close the drug store on Saturday and we're not open on Sunday. We'll be gone those two days and be back home for business as usual on Monday."

"Congratulations! That is great news. Now for a toast." Beulah raised her tea goblet high. "To George and Cornelia. May you have a long and happy marriage."

"To George and Cornelia," the rest of the guests echoed.

"Clara?" Beulah nodded toward her.

"We told Libby today and she's been a very good girl to keep our secret." Clara hugged the daughter sitting between her and Briar. "We'd like to announce that we'll be having a baby in the summer. Libby will be getting a brother or sister."

Beulah raised her glass again. "Wonderful news! To the next generation."

Everyone followed suit.

"We weren't really so surprised," Tilly whispered. "It's been written all over you for weeks."

"I know but I wanted an announcement and Beulah said she wanted a big party tonight so we decided to save the news," Clara whispered back.

"And now for my announcement," Beulah said. "Actually it's mine and Dulcie's together. We've decided to retire. Cornelia will be moving out at the end of the week. Nellie is going tomorrow. Olivia already married and left us not long after Clara did. Bessie took off on her own without waiting for me to go to eternity with her. Just leaves me and Dulcie to rattle around in this big old house. Oh, we could rent the rooms to oil men anytime we wanted, but I don't want to hunt up a robe every time I have to visit the necessary room at night. Don't blush, Julius. Women do have to do those things. So Dulcie and I put our head together and decided to retire. We've bought the Wesley home. That little white two bedroom house on the block behind the drug store. That way we'll be close enough to town to do our shopping and we won't have to run up and down steps anymore."

"But what about the Morning Glory Inn?" Clara asked.

"That's where Doctor Addison comes in. I've got more money than Midas and you all know it. I don't need what this house would bring if I sold it, so I'm deeding it over to the city. But, don't look so stunned. The whole lot of you act like you just saw me eat a live toad frog. There are conditions to my deed. First of all it has to be used as a hospital and medical clinic. There's rooms aplenty upstairs for a small hospital and the living room can be a waiting room, the dining room could be for surgery and the kitchen, well, every hospital has to have a kitchen. Briar has offered to outfit the surgery room, compliments of Rose Oil Company. Only thing we need is a doctor to run the thing. We'd be honored if you'd be the doctor we're looking for, Addison."

Silence prevailed. Addison had to fight the urge to pinch her arm. Surely she was dreaming. She chanced a glance across the table at Tucker who kept his eyes on his plate. Could she do it? Run a hospital single handedly? It was a challenge. It scared her half to death.

"Well?" Beulah asked. "Dulcie and I will be out by next Monday. You can stay here in one of the empty rooms until then."

"She doesn't want to live in Healdton," Tucker mumbled.

"Why?" Beulah asked. "Healdton is just as good as any other place for her to get her feet wet in the profession. We're friendly and we're needing a doctor. What do you say, Addison?"

"Outfitting a surgery room? That's expensive."

"The last doctor who was here has his equipment on the market," Briar said. "If you will stay, I'll buy it. Besides Clara is having a baby. It will be an investment. She likes and trusts you."

"Please," Olivia begged. "We need you."

"Then yes, yes, yes, and thank you, thank you. I have my money from taking care of Tucker. I'll use every dime of it to get things started." She couldn't wipe the smile off her face or stop her eyes from welling up. Be damned to whatever Tucker thought. He could go to Ardmore for his medical care. She had just been of-fered the moon and she wasn't going to turn it down.

"I'd guess after supper you big strong men better take her trunks out of Tilly's car and tote them up to Clara's old room," Beulah said. "Next week we'll run an article in the local paper and one in the Ardmoreite telling the whole area that Dr. Addison Carter has hung out her shingle in Healdton, Oklahoma. Cornelia, you reckon you could write that up for us?"

"I'll do it before George and I leave on Friday. I can't remember a time when I've been so happy. Every thing is so . . . so . . . there are no words. It's like a cloud of happiness is floating in this room." Cornelia's smile was so bright it lit the room like a thousand candles.

Addison looked at Tucker. His cloud wasn't one of happiness, more like impending doom. The poor man had thought he'd be rid of her and now she was staying in his town, treating his friends, a woman running a hospital. From the look on his face, it was almost more than he could bear.

Actually, Tucker was glad there was another genera-tion on the way. He was happy for both his girl cousins and their happy marriages. He was only a little bit jeal-ous of George and Cornelia and very glad to see Nellie take her opinions to Tishomingo.

Healdton desperately needed a hospital and a doctor

so he could appreciate that. It was Addison. He didn't think he could tolerate her in his circles and she'd be there. She'd already made fast friends with Olivia. That meant she'd be at church every Sunday some woman wasn't birthing a child or some kid hadn't stuffed beans up her nose. Tilly and Clara thought she was truly some kind of angel in human form just because she took good care of him. So they'd be inviting her to every family function.

Hopefully there'd be lots of births and he'd supply the beans if the ladies out in Ragtown, or Wirt as they called it now, would leave them slung under the kitchen table. That way Addison would be so busy she wouldn't have time to come out of the clinic because with the way he was feeling right then, he couldn't guarantee that he'd be a gentleman. He yearned to kiss her again and smell the rose scent she wore.

Life sure took some topsy-turvy turns, Addison thought as she laced her fingers behind her head that night. A part of her still felt like she did in medical school when she lived in a boarding house. It wasn't nearly as nice as the Morning Glory but she could hear the snores of the other ladies in the rooms down the hallway, just like she could right then. She still had trouble believing her good luck even yet. To think she'd been ready to march into the recruiting office tomorrow morning. Instead, Briar was taking her to look at the medical equipment the doctor had for sale.

She couldn't sleep so she pulled the light chain and took pen and paper from her chest and crawled back up in bed. She used the Sears catalog she found on the vanity for a lap desk and wrote a long letter to her brother and father. Starting by apologizing for not keeping in touch, but explaining that she'd had a private practice job for the past six weeks that kept her busy, she went on to tell them that she'd been asked to start a hospital in Healdton. She would be the only doctor and for a while, until she could afford help, would run it alone. Her excitement flowed through the ink and even when the words were on paper and the envelope sealed and addressed, she still didn't believe this had happened to her.

Using a cane, Tucker carefully made his way a slow step at a time to his bedroom. If he fell, there'd be no one to rush out of the bedroom and rescue him. He was alone in his house for the first time since he fell off the barn. What he'd thought would be pure ecstasy was actually a little frightening. The 'what if's' plagued him. What if he fell? What if he couldn't drive the truck tomorrow morning to get the chores done? What if that heifer really did go into labor and he needed help to pull the calf? On and on the fears chased good common sense while he undressed. He didn't have to bother with pajamas tonight. That was exciting. He could sleep in his long johns and not worry about what the woman doctor thought of it.

He opened the door across the hallway from his. Her smell lingered in the room. A clean, no nonsense soapy odor, mixed with a hint of roses. She'd bent over him so many times—checking his heart, his temperature, making sure his pillows were right—that he'd memorized the smell of her hair. He sat down at the vanity and looked in the mirror. The same old Tucker Anderson stared back at him who'd been looking at him for years. Nothing had changed on the outside but he had to look away to avoid the haunted look in his own eyes. There was a kinky red hair lying on the vanity. One she'd missed when she did the final cleaning. It must have fallen out of her hair brush. He picked it up and held it up to the light. Bright coppery red, curly, and not a bit over six inches long. Her hair color fit her. Bold enough to plow right into a man's world whether he wanted her there or not. Sassier than any woman he'd ever known. Short, like the new modern woman image, leaving the woman of yesterday behind and pressing on to the woman of tomorrow.

He admired her even if he didn't agree with her. He moved to the bed and turned back the covers. It was his house and he could sleep in any room he pleased. He dropped his pants and shirt on the floor on top of his shoes and socks and slipped beneath the sheets, drawing the quilts up to his chin. The pillow case smelled more like her than the room. He sunk his face down into it and remembered her saying the mattress was the softest one in the house. It was. So much so, he just might change rooms and take the master bedroom for his own. After all, he was master of Evening Star, of this house and of his own heart and mind. At least that's what he kept reminding himself as he fell asleep and dreamed of Addison Carter for the first time.

Chapter Twelve

Valentine's Day ushered in bright sunshine and unseasonably warm weather—seventy degrees by the middle of the day. People stirred away from the warm fires and out into town even though it was only Thursday. There'd be plenty more blustery days when they'd be confined inside. They wandered about slowly, taking time to stop and visit, to have a cup of coffee, hot chocolate or iced tea at the drug store, to stop and gawk at the Morning Glory Inn which sported a sign on the door that said it was now the Morning Glory Hospital and Clinic.

Addison took advantage of the bright sunshine by opening the windows and airing out the whole house. What had been the living room was now a waiting area with filing cabinets and a desk. The dining room had been converted to an examination and surgery room combined. Someday she'd have a small desk and receptionist set up in the foyer and a staff of nurses, at least one for each eight hour shift. Until that time, she was chief cook, bottle washer, doctor, nurse—in charge of everything from taking temperature to emptying bed pans. It wasn't scary or intimidating, rather exhilarating. In her wildest dreams, she'd never thought she'd have her own hospital.

Olivia rapped on the open kitchen door but didn't wait for an invitation. "Hey, Doc, where are you?" She set a quart of soup on the table and picked an apron from a hook beside the stove.

"In the exam room," Addison called out. "Come on in."

"I've got the afternoon free again. Brought soup for your supper. Julius is off to Wirt to see about the new church they're building. Beautiful day like this, they might get some work done. So what are we doing?"

"I'm washing down this table. There's enough dust on it to infect a patient."

"Hand me a rag and I'll help. You think all this stuff will be clean enough for the grand opening next week?"

"With your help, I do," Addison said. "The waiting room is ready. The rooms upstairs look really good. This is the room everyone will want to see. It's where the actual doctoring goes on and it's what will interest them so I want it sparkling clean. After they all leave I'll wash it all again to get the germs off that they bring."

"Don't tell anyone that," Olivia advised.

"Why?"

"Because they wouldn't understand. Hey, I got a short note from Nellie this morning in the mail. Guess what she's doing?"

"Teaching already, I would suppose." Addison answered but from the look on Olivia's face, she wouldn't be surprised at anything.

"No, she got over to Tishomingo and the job doesn't really begin for two weeks. So she and her sister caught a train to Washington D. C. They're going to join the Silent Sentinels and picket the White House. I could hardly believe it even if it is Nellie. To sit back and fuss about something is so different from actually doing it. Did you read this morning's paper? The Silent Sentinels have been picketing day and night for over a year. They take off on Sunday only. Those girls really mean business."

"What's Julius think of that?" Addison kept working as she talked.

"Oh, he thinks they're a bunch of radical, crazy women. He says times are changing and that women will have rights someday without all this crazy stuff. I just can't believe Nellie would have the nerve to do that, is all."

"It takes the radicals to bring about changes. I'm glad President Wilson announced his support last month. He'll take a beating for it, but it's good to have the president on our side."

"It took a year of women picketing to get him to give his support. They were talking in the paper about Lucy Burns and Katherine Morey being hauled into jail because they were demonstrating, and some of the suffragettes have actually been beaten and tied up. All kinds of bad things. They're saying the president is going to outlaw punishing them when they take them to jail. I don't think I'd want the president's job. Trying to wage a war on one side, appease the suffragettes, do a military draft, and that's not even mentioning all the tax changes."

"What's your honest opinion about women's rights?" Addison asked.

"I think we'll get rights someday. I don't think I could join the Silent Sentinels but I appreciate what they're doing for us, even if they are fanatical. I suppose the most extreme thing I ever did was leave home and work in the bank. For me, that was a big step of independence. I lived alone, went out with guys I wanted even if they were wild, and married Julius even when everyone thought I was making a mistake. What's the most drastic thing you ever did?" Olivia scrubbed inside a cabinet where Addison planned to keep medicine.

"Going to medical school and becoming a doctor. I'm not one to march on the White House lawn, but rather to simply be what I want to be, in spite of the attitude of others. Guess you're kind of showing your fanatic side by coming here to help me every day. There'll be those who will criticize you for that, I'm sure."

"They condemned me for working, for dating oil men, for dancing and taking a sip of moonshine, and then for marrying a preacher. I don't guess I can please all of them all of the time. You are my friend and I like helping you. Tell the truth, I get bored at the parsonage. I was used to working all day. Somedays I wish I still had a job," Olivia said.

"Are you serious? What would Julius think of you working?"

"I'm not real sure what he'd think. He tends to be very conservative and if he didn't want me to work, I don't suppose I would," Olivia answered.

"If you want a job, I could hire you part-time here at the first. I need someone to help me clean, cook and keep the records. We could work together. I'd even train you to do nursing duties if you want."

Olivia stopped cleaning and sat down in a chair. "Are you serious?"

"I am. I made a lot of money taking care of Tucker. I can't hire you full-time, but I'd sure like some help. You could choose your days and your hours. Afternoons would suit me fine. Three days a week, maybe."

"I'll take it. At least I will after I talk to Julius. I don't think he'll have a bit of problem with that since I'm here that much anyway. Thank you, so much, Addy."

"It's me who should be thanking you. Reckon you could start by baking for the grand opening? I want to serve cookies and punch and the two of us could be hostesses together."

Olivia jumped up and hugged Addison. "You bet I can. I can't wait to answer Nellie's letter now. She'll be so surprised that I'm working with you in the new hospital. It might not be as earth-shattering as carrying a sign on the White House lawn, but it's a step in showing women everywhere that we can have careers and make a home too. I'll be doing my little part."

Clara caught them in the kitchen at noon, eating soup and discussing just how they would set up the file cabinets to keep accurate records of the steady patients and finances, as well. She told them she'd planned to stay at home that day and work on the layette but the warmth of the sun, the promise of spring not too far around the corner and cabin fever caused her to dress Libby and come into town.

Clara removed her coat and hung it over the back of a kitchen chair, poured herself a cup of coffee and Libby a glass of milk. "So what are you two doing? We couldn't stay in today. Libby and I had lunch with Briar at the hotel and we're going to the store to buy cotton for baby nightgowns later. We may even have ice cream at the drug store. Seems lately that I'm craving it all the time."

"Me, too," Libby piped up. "Momma is having me a baby sister because ice cream is my favorite thing in the whole world and my baby sister likes it, too and she's telling Momma to eat it so she can sneak a bite. Did I tell you that my baby sister is going to be Susanna. I like that name. Daddy doesn't like Susanna but I think I can talk him into it."

"I bet you can," Olivia giggled. "Addy has offered me a part-time job helping her right here. You think Julius will object?"

"I think Julius would lay down across a cow pile to keep you from walking in it. He's a changed man since y'all married. Even his sermons aren't so hellfire and brimstone anymore," Clara said.

"You're right. I used to hate it when he preached on moonshine or dancing every single week. It's nice to hear something positive," Olivia agreed.

Addison finished her soup. "Since you're here, you can be my first patient. The exam room is clean and I'll give you a check-up. See if everything is where it's supposed to be."

"I'd love that. I was going to make an appointment for after the grand opening." Clara picked up her coffee and carried it with her. "My skirts are too tight. My blouses are busting the buttons and my breasts are tender. Are those good signs?"

"The best. Everything is growing as it should. Now Libby, if you'll stay in here and keep Olivia company, we're going into this other room. We'll be back real soon."

"I can do that," Libby said seriously. "Olivia, since we're going to visit can I have some coffee with lots of milk and three spoons of sugar."

"I could fix that right up if it's all right with your mommy." Olivia suppressed a smile.

"Do you want that or ice cream?" Clara asked.

"Both ice cream and coffee are too much sugar for a little girl."

"Then I'm waiting for ice cream. This milk will do just fine if I can have ice cream after a while," Libby declared without hesitation, her black curls dancing as she shook her head to the idea of coffee.

"First we'll weigh you." Addison pointed to the scales.

"Oh, I hate scales," Clara said.

"All women hate them but this way I can keep a close watch on your weight and it will help me take care of you better." Addison shoved the balance back and forth until she got it to settle right in the middle, then wrote down the number. "I'll take an oath and seal it in blood that I'll never tell."

"Now that's a doctor worth having," Clara said. "What next?"

"I want you to step behind that screen and remove all your clothing except for your underpants and put on a gown. They open in the back usually, but I want you to leave it open in the front like a kimono robe."

Clara tossed her clothing up on the screen and sighed when she unfastened the button on her skirt. "I've never been to a doctor other than for a sore throat occasionally when I was a child so this is all new to me. I think it's time for maternity things but I'm only three months and everyone will say I'm silly."

"If your skirts are too tight then wear something comfortable. I don't care if it's overalls, just don't bind up your stomach. It's not healthy."

Clara hurried to the table and hopped up on it, her bare feet barely touching the cold wooden floor. "I remember why I wore shoes all the time when I lived here. This floor is freezing even if it is a nice day outside."

"Got good warm rugs at your house?" Addison fixed the stethoscope in her ears.

"Oh, yes. You'll have to come by when you have time. I know you are busy but now that Tucker doesn't take every waking minute, you can make time to visit us. Now what do I do?"

"Lay on your back. What I'm going to do is listen to your heartbeat and hope I can pick up one for the baby."

Clara's pale blue eyes were filled with wonder. "Can you do that?"

"We can try. It's pretty early. You say you think you are three months?"

"Maybe four. I haven't felt any flutters yet and Beulah says that comes about half way through."

"Be very quiet," Addison said.

Clara's heart sounded healthy. Her tummy was barely protruding but her waistline had thickened. Addison moved the stethoscope down and with very little effort picked up the baby's heartbeat. Loud and clear, it sounded like a very healthy baby. She counted the beats and looked at the clock on the wall at the same time.

"Well?" Clara asked.

"You listen. Just be very still. You put these in your ears and I'll keep this right here so we won't lose the beat," Addison said.

Clara gasped when she heard the steady thump. "Can Libby hear it?"

"Of course," Addison nodded. "Hold this until I get back."

She opened the kitchen door. "Libby, come in here. We want you to hear something."

Clara was still beaming when Addison carefully sat Libby beside her and fixed the earpieces so Libby could hear. "That is our new baby's little heart," Clara explained. "That means it's growing like it's supposed to."

"Momma, how's it going to get out?" Libby flipped her head from side to side and dislodged the stethoscope. "And how long until she's big enough for me to play with her?"

"We'll talk about all how she gets out when you're older and I expect you'll find ways to play with her from the time she's born," Clara said.

"You can get dressed now," Addison told Clara. "I'll see you every two weeks from now on just to keep a close check on things. Briar would have me drawn and quartered if anything happened to you or this child."

Libby ran back into the kitchen to tell Olivia what she'd heard. Addison wrote down everything on a brand new record for Clara, her first official patient. Clara left the top button open on her skirt and vowed she'd buy or sew maternity clothing that very weekend.

"Clara, are you going to be disappointed if this baby is a boy?" Addison asked.

"No, I don't care if it's a boy or girl, long as it's a healthy child. Briar would dance on air if it happened to be a boy."

"What about Libby? None of us would want to see her disappointed."

"Libby won't care once it's here. Are you trying to tell me something?"

"Nothing concrete but that baby's heartbeat sure sounded like a big old lazy boy to me. Girls are usually faster. It's nothing you can take to the bank."

"Then I'll stop putting lace on every pink blanket and make sure there are boy things in the layette," Clara smiled. "Secretly, I want a boy for Briar."

Addison walked Clara and Libby to the front door and watched them go together hand in hand down the street toward the drug store. Someday she wanted a daughter and she wanted her to be just as inquisitive as Libby—one who'd ask questions even if they weren't proper and who was so comfortable that she'd talk about anything. They were out of sight before she started back inside the house.

A car horn brought her up short and she looked over her shoulder. Tucker's truck came to a screeching halt right in front of the hospital. He bailed out and literally ran across the yard and onto the porch. It wasn't until he was three feet from her that she noticed the towel wrapped around his hand. Blood dripped through it onto his pant leg.

"What have you done? Get into the exam room and let me take a look."

"I was opening a bag of feed with my pocket knife and it slipped. Got me from the thumb to the wrist. I guess it'll need stitches," he said.

She motioned for him to sit on the table and carefully removed the towel. It was his left hand this time. At least the other one had healed or he'd be in need of a private care provider again. "That's a nasty cut, Tucker. It does need stitches and lots of them. I'm going to deaden it and it'll hurt like hell. Get ready for it. But once it's numb, you won't feel a thing."

"Don't waste the deadening medicine. I can take it," he growled.

"I don't work that way. I'll numb it and then sew it up. It heals better that way in my opinion. Bet it really pained you to have to come see me, didn't it?"

"Oh, yes." He gritted his teeth when he saw her drawing a needle full of medicine and heading toward his hand. "Hell's bells, that hurts like sin."

"And how bad does sin hurt, Tucker?" She kept talking, hopefully to take his mind off the wound. It was deeper than the one she'd stitched on his right palm. Cleaner, by a long shot, but deeper. "What had you been doing with that knife?"

"Cleaned my toenails last night." He said through clenched teeth. Cold, clammy sweat covered his face.

"That's just great. I'd clean it good anyway, but I'll

do an extra job before I start sewing it up. You've already had a tetanus shot so you won't have to endure one of those. Do you feel that?" She poked the needle down inside the cut.

"No, but the room is spinning," he admitted.

"Lay down. I don't need a big horse of a man like you sprawled out on the floor with a head wound as well as a cut hand. Here. Easy now. That's the way. Right flat on your back. Don't shut your eyes. Keep them open and look at the ceiling. Focus on anything in the room, but don't shut your eyes. If you do, all you'll think about is the pain. I've put another round of medicine in the cut and I'm going to start sewing now. I'll make the stitches very close together so it won't scar too badly." She talked the whole time she worked because she believed that soothed the patient.

She could stitch in her sleep. She'd sworn sometimes she did just that when she was interning in Little Rock, Arkansas. After twenty-four hours with no sleep and living on black coffee to stay awake, there were times when she wondered if she'd really sewn up a kid's arm or leg or if she'd dreamed it. She'd learned by practicing for hours and hours on eggplants. Each intern had their own favorite item to slit open and sew shut; hers was the eggplant because it felt more like skin.

"You always been accident prone?" She asked.

"No, never had an accident in my life, other than skinning up my knees or that one time when I was trying to fly. I took Momma's table cloth to the back porch roof and crashed and burned in the rose bushes. I didn't break anything but Momma nearly broke her hand on my bottom for tearing up her roses. I was glad I was only going to be a plain old bird. An eagle would have flown from the attic window."

"Looks like you are making up for lost time," Addison said.

"No, it's you. You came to town the very day I fell off the roof. You are bad luck for me."

"Then I expect you'll have lots of bad luck because I'm staying. There's the last stitch. Thirteen. It was deep and long. I want to see you tomorrow to change the bandage and again on Saturday. If it looks good after forty-eight hours then I'll see you in a week, and then take the stitches out in two weeks. Be still while I put a bandage on it."

"How much do I owe you?" He asked when she'd finished. The room did a couple of loops before he got it under control.

"You want to pay the whole bill now or just pay for today and for each visit as you come in?"

"Pay it up front and be done with it." He was already reaching inside the bib pocket of his overalls.

"Five dollars," she said.

"Fair enough." He pulled out his wallet and handed it to her. "Take out five. I can't do it with one hand."

"You going to need a full-time doctor again?" She teased as she withdrew five dollars.

"No, I am not! I can take care of myself."

"I'll see you tomorrow. Want to make an appointment or just drop in?"

"I'll be in sometime in the afternoon," he said. "Need to buy feed."

"You are not to be lifting anything with that hand for two weeks, Tucker Anderson. After I look at your hand, I'll go with you and unload the feed. Besides I need to check on my baby calf."

"It's not your calf. And there ain't been a day dawned yet that I let a woman do my work."

"I'd say about six weeks of days have come and gone that a woman did your work," she reminded him.

"You were paid help. That don't count."

"Then you're going to get some paid help for the next two weeks. No lifting hay bales. I better not see a hay hook in your hands. Not a bit of pressure on that cut or it'll split wide open and infect."

"You are serious, aren't you?" He said. When he stood up she barely came to his shoulder so all he could see was big green eyes and all that unruly red hair.

"Very. Hire a hobo. Or someone looking for winter work. Get Ford to help you with chores. You can take care of yourself and cook, but you cannot lift."

"Don't suppose I'd better be pulling a calf if that heifer goes into labor, had I?

"Don't even suggest it."

"I'm right back to square one," he moaned. "I'll hire some part-time help if it'll keep you off the Evening Star and out of my business.

"It will but I'll be coming to see my calf Sunday." She wondered why she was insisting on going where she wasn't wanted.

"Going to walk?"

"No, I'm going to ride home with you after church, see my calf and go to Clara's for dinner."

"We're eating at Tilly's this week so you'll be eating alone if you go to Clara's," he said.

"Then you can bring me back to town after I see the calf and you can go to Tilly's."

"What if I say no?"

"Are you?"

"Yes, I am. I'm not going to be seen driving away from church with you. Do you realize what people will say? That we're courting."

"Well, Lord save your precious reputation, Tucker Anderson. I'll drop by sometime and see the calf. I don't have to see you when I do. Just promise me you really will get someone to come help do the chores until the hand is healed."

"I promise," he nodded.

She scrubbed down the table and floor after he'd gone, taking out her frustrations in a flurry of hard work. That man could rile her quicker than her brother and father combined. He could give her a case of pure old mad faster than those guys in medical school. It was a miracle she hadn't murdered him in those six weeks she'd lived at Evening Star.

The very thought of the farm's name brought a

yearning to see it again. To feel the winter wind on her face at daybreak. To hear the cows bawling and Bill barking. To feel the soft warmth of the dog's fur in the early morning when he begged to have his neck scratched. She'd go back sometime just to prove her point to Tucker; to let him know she wouldn't be pushed around or told what to do.

"Tucker gone?" Olivia poked her head in the door.

"How'd you know he was here?"

"I heard you two arguing. I decided to lay low and make cookies. Got two batches of oatmeal ones done while you sewed him up. Ya'll fight like Briar and Clara did when he lived here, but so far you haven't been as bad as Ford and Tilly. Me and Julius never did much fighting. Seemed like we fit together from the beginning. Guess some folks has to work through a lot before they listen to their hearts."

"My heart says it would like to shake that man until his teeth rattle," Addison said.

Chapter Thirteen

Sunday morning found Addison sitting beside Olivia on the front pew of the church. Julius preached on being kind and considerate of others even when it wasn't a holiday like Valentine's Day. Addison's mind wandered instead of paying attention to the sermon. She'd already had several patients but nothing serious enough to require staying in the hospital. Most had paid the dollar a visit right up front; some had given her a chicken or eggs. One man offered a small hog for her to come to his house and deliver a baby, but she had to decline since she had no place to keep livestock. They finally settled on a ham which she gave to Olivia, but the books showed that he'd paid in full.

Every attendant appeared to have a pew they liked and those who sat in the back filed out first. After services

Addison and Olivia were among the last to leave the church. When she finally shook Julius' hand and stepped out into the nippy morning air, Tilly was waiting.

"Thought you'd taken up residence in there." Tilly looped her arm in Addison's. "Dinner is at my place today. Julius and Olivia are coming and you are too. I've invited the new school teacher, also. Her name is Katy Hillerman and she's riding with Clara. She just got into town yesterday. She's rented the house right beside the school. Come on, you can go with me. Ford can go with Tucker."

"But what if—" Addison started.

"We'll stop by Morning Glory and put a sign on the door. That's what the old doc did when he left the office. We always knew where to find him and he didn't have to stay inside all the time."

There was barely room to seat everyone around the table so elbows had to be tucked in and shoulders touched. Tucker sat between Addison and the new school teacher, Katy, who was quite taken with Tucker. She hung on his every word, batted her lashes at him and talked in a soft Alabama drawl. Addison wanted to reach around behind Tucker's back and jerk a clump of black hair from Katy's head.

Addison excused herself in the middle of the meal and went up to the bathroom where she gave the red haired doctor on the other side of the mirror a severe lecture. There was no reason why Katy shouldn't flirt with Tucker. He was an eligible bachelor, even a desirable one. So if he wanted to be taken in by her airs, then it wasn't a bit of Addison's business. When she slipped into her seat again, dessert was being passed. Three tiered chocolate cake and pecan pie. She opted for half a piece of each.

"And you say your grandmother's name was Katy? Isn't that a coincidence that my name is the same? I bet she was a lovely lady," Katy said. "No, no, Clara, please pass it on, darlin', I just couldn't force myself to eat another bite. The meal has been delicious and I do love chocolate but I must not indulge or I'll look like the side of a barn."

"Not much chance of that," Tucker said, more to aggravate Addison that to compliment Katy. "And yes, my grandmother was Katy Evening Star Hawk Anderson. She's the one who inspired the name of my ranch. My mother loved her so much that she named the ranch for her."

"How delightful. You must show me your ranch some time. I do love a nice stroll around a working ranch. There's so many wonderous things to see."

"I'd be delighted," Tucker said.

He'd teach Addison to think she had free reign to come and go on the Evening Star when she wanted. He'd invite another woman right in her presence.

"Tell me, what do you think of the suffragette movement?" He looked into Katy's eyes and deliberately ignored Addison.

"Oh, I think they are a bunch of radical women who

are harming the gender more than they could ever help it. A woman should know her place and stay in it. Men have taken care of things for years and years and it's worked. Why try to fix something that's not broken?" Katy smiled.

Anger shot from one ear through Addison's brain and out the other side like an electrical current. Her face turned bright red; her hands knotted into fists. She glanced across the table at Olivia who bit the inside of her lower lip.

"Then you don't agree with women working outside the home? I would have thought, you being a school teacher and all, that you would have different views," Olivia said.

"Oh, women have to support themselves, when there's no one else to help them," Katy said demurely, lowering her dark lashes. "But once a woman is married, there's no reason for her to forsake the family by having a job. I'm surprised my colleague is a married woman. I'd really hoped to work with another single lady."

"I see," Olivia said.

"Then in your opinion, I could be a doctor but if I married, then I should give up my profession?" Addison asked.

"Yes, ma'am, that's what I think, but then I trained to be a teacher but only until I can find my knight in shining armor. Like every little southern princess, I'm waiting for him to come along on a big white horse and carry me off to live happy ever after."

"Honey, you might have a long wait. There's precious few white horses and even less knights with their armor all shined up in Healdton, Oklahoma," Tilly told her.

Katy looked right at Tucker. "Oh, I don't know. I bet there's more than you think."

Olivia caught Addison's eye and winked. Something wasn't right even if neither of them could put their finger on it. Following dinner, the ladies all gathered in the kitchen to help with the clean up—all but Katy, who insisted Tucker give her a little tour of Tilly's farm so the wonderful meal wouldn't put her to sleep.

Addison dried plates, put them into the cupboard and fumed. Olivia washed dishes and kept a straight face. It was as plain as the snout on a pig's face that Addison had feelings for Tucker and even plainer that he was smitten, but neither of them were ready to admit such a thing.

"Well, what do you think of her?" Clara asked.

"She's a fake. Where'd the school board find her, anyway?" Addison asked.

"Got her resume from Austin, Texas. Strange how it happened. Nellie and Cornelia both quit and the lady from Wirt applied for a job right about that time. Then the next day this resume came in the mail. They took one look at it and had their minds made up by the time she got here on the train. All she had to do was open her mouth and bat those lashes and she had them in her pocket," Clara said.

"Something's not right," Olivia said.

"Yep, you're all right, but what could it be? She's twenty-eight years old. Been teaching eight years. Started in Alabama. Wound up in Austin. Everything seems to be on the up and up," Tilly said.

"Things ain't always what they seem," Addison said. "That woman is not twenty-eight. She's forty if she's a day."

"Forty?" Olivia gasped. "That's older than my mother. How could she be that old?"

"She's got her ways," Addison said.

"Jealous are we?" Olivia giggled.

"No," Addison said entirely too fast.

They'd barely finished the job when Katy and Tucker rushed in the back door, giggling and holding their hands over their heads. It had begun to rain and they'd run from the barn back to the house. Katy excused herself and asked if she might use the rest room to redo her hair. Addison kept her mouth shut, but it was no easy feat; one look at the woman said it was her make-up that needed touching up, not her hair.

Tucker joined the men in the living room. He was quite proud of himself. Addison Carter was so angry she looked as if every freckle on her nose was ready to pop off. That was good. Tucker wanted her mad; hoped she stayed that way so long it fried her brain and she forgot the way out to the Evening Star.

"So what did you find out about the school teacher?" Ford teased, his brown eyes twinkling.

"Nothing more than she said at the dinner table.

She's all right. I wouldn't want to get mixed up with her though. Something ain't right. She talks and she's all sweet and gushy, but her eyes don't back up her stories. I don't know what it is, but I'll be steering clear of her."

"Glad to hear it," Briar said. "There's something familiar about her, but I can't put my finger on it. I don't know where in the world my path would have crossed an Alabama school teacher's."

"Oh, Tucker, darlin', if you'd give me a ride home, I think I'd best be going. Tomorrow morning is my first day and I have preparations to do." Katy poked her head into the living room.

All three men blushed, hoping against hope that she hadn't overheard what they were talking about. Tucker jumped up a second too quickly and agreed to take her home just as the women and Libby joined them from the kitchen. Addison glared at him and even if he hadn't been coerced into taking the woman home, he would have offered anyway.

"Thank you Tilly for sharing your home and family with me today. It's so nice to be included in a community like this. I'm sure I'm going to love it here," Katy said.

"Are you going to stay a whole year?" Libby asked.

"Oh, honey, I may stay a lifetime." Katy looped her arm through Tucker's.

"I hope she don't," Libby said when they'd shut the front door. "I don't like that woman. She looks at me mean."

"Libby!" Clara said.

"Well, she does, Momma. I was up there in that room where Aunt Tilly keeps things for me to play with while she was in the bathroom and I heard her talking and she didn't sound like she did at the table and when she come out the door and saw me she looked at me mean."

Briar drew his daughter into his lap. "Out of the mouths of babes. What do you say, we talk Uncle Ford into a game of checkers and then we'd better go home and get a Sunday afternoon nap?"

"I can beat you." Libby narrowed her eyes at Ford.

"As sleepy as I am, you probably can," Ford laughed.

Katy couldn't have asked for things to be going one bit better than they were. If she'd paid someone to get her an introduction into Tucker Anderson's family, she couldn't have slipped into such wonderfully good luck. She rode beside Tucker in the pickup truck and counted her blessings, having to hold her hands in her lap to keep from clapping with joy.

"Tell me how you hurt your hand, darlin'," she crooned.

"I was opening a bag of feed and slit it open with my knife. I'm just glad it was my left hand. The right one has healed up real good but several weeks ago I had an accident; I fell off the barn roof. I broke my leg when I landed, and hit the shovel with my right hand. Guess I've turned accident prone this winter."

"Surely not." She hid a giggle behind her hand.

"Tilly and Clara hired Dr. Carter to take care of me," he said bluntly.

"I thought she looked at you too familiar. You do know she's got a terrible crush on you, don't you?"

"Addison? That's a laugh. She and I don't get along at all. She's bossy as hell, pardon my language, ma'am. That's not the kind of talk a school teacher would hear. But she is sassy and she's a doctor and I don't like women doctors."

Katy moved over in the seat and put her hand on Tucker's knee. "I'm glad. It's a shame the way some women get so high-minded and think they can take the place of a man."

"You got that right. A woman should keep herself for her fellow on the big white horse like you said." Tucker wondered exactly what this woman was doing, resting her hand on his knee. He'd be glad to get her home and be rid of her.

When they arrived at the little shotgun house beside the school, he parked as close to the door as he could, ran around the car and opened the door for Katy. "I'll be seeing you around, I'm sure. Good luck tomorrow on your first day of school."

Katy dashed up onto the porch out of the rain. "Well, thank you so much, Tucker. Join me for a cup of coffee to take the chill off?"

"No thanks. I'd best be getting on home. The man I've got hired to help with chores will be there shortly."

"Then goodbye." She waved sweetly, turned around and fell into a heap right in front of the door.

Tucker hurried up two steps and picked her up, opened the door and carried her inside. Everything was in disarray—unpacked boxes everywhere, clothing piled on a rocking chair in the living room, a double bed in the room right ahead. When he gently laid her on it, she fluttered her eyes and clung to him.

"Don't leave me, darlin'. Not until I can stand up and not faint again. That is so scary when I do that. You won't tell the school board members, will you? I didn't tell them that I sometimes have these little spells." She sat up and pressed her bosom into his chest.

"Can I get you some tea or water?"

Her voice was hollow. "Hot tea would be so nice. The kitchen is right through there." She pointed at the door on the other side of the bedroom.

The stove was old but it appeared to draw just fine when he lit the wood. He opened the back door to find someone had filled the wood box so she should be fine for a few days. He felt obligated to stay long enough to see her able to stand on her own two feet, but what he really wanted to do was run away as fast as he could.

In a few minutes the teapot whistled. Avoiding all the piles of boxes and clothing, he carried it to the bedroom where she was propped up on pillows. She'd taken the pins from her hair and it lay in soft waves over one shoulder all the way to her waist.

"Those pins were making my head hurt. Please go

fix yourself a cup, also. I'll be fine in just a moment and thank you so much for staying with me. It's so scary when that happens and I'm all alone."

"I'm sure it is. Maybe I will have some tea while I wait a few more minutes to be sure you are well again."

Anything to get out of this room with you. I've got a feeling you're up to no good. People in town would have your job if they knew you had a man in your room and you in the bed with your hair down. School teachers don't do that. I'll have to tell Tilly or Clara to come talk to you about the way things are done in Oklahoma.

Katy waited until she heard him in the kitchen before she dumped the contents of a capsule into the tea and stirred it with her finger. Just a sip or two would put him out until tomorrow morning. She hadn't figured on such good fortune. She might never have to step into that schoolroom and pretend to be a teacher at all.

You sweet rich naïve man. I promise to make you happy for a few weeks and then you'll have another one of your accidents. Only this one will be fatal.

"Feeling better?" He sat down in a high backed chair as far from the bed as he could.

"Yes, darlin', I surely am. But this tea has gone luke-warm. Could you trade with me? Seems like it helps me regain strength if it's really hot and yours is steaming." She tucked her chin down coyly.

He swapped with her. He'd drink the water from the mud puddle in front of the hotel where the horses were hitched if he could just get out of that house gracefully.

Every sound made him jump, fearing someone would catch him in there. He sipped the tea; it didn't seem so lukewarm to him. It did have a bitter taste but that could have easily been the brand.

One second he was gulping it down as fast as he could; the next, Katy was somewhere in a fog. He could see her form in the bed but no amount of squinting could bring her in focus. The walls began to move toward him. When they touched his shoulders he fell out of the chair and darkness covered him.

Katy let him lay there while she unpacked the boxes and set the empty ones out on the porch. She hung up dresses, blouses and skirts, all brand new and conservative like a school teacher would wear. She hated every piece of the clothing. She was used to wearing silk and fur, not cotton and wool. Her pert little nose turned as she hung them neatly in the wardrobe. It actually snarled when she folded cotton underwear and put them into the bureau drawer. She had to step over him to straighten the kitchen and again to get the living room in shape. After all, when they came tomorrow morning, it should look as if she were really a school teacher.

When the place was in good condition, she attempted to haul his snoring body to the bed. She grunted and groaned as she worked to lift his dead weight. She had him in a death grip under the arms and twice he slipped before she finally got a portion of him onto the bed. "Dammit, man. You're about the heaviest

one I've had to get from the floor to the bed." The soft
southern tone was replaced with a flat accent.

Once she had him stretched out on the bed, the rest
of the job was easy. She undressed him, slipped the
covers up to his chest, laid his head on the pillow and
tousled his dark hair. While he slept peacefully, she
went to the kitchen and prepared a sandwich and
scanned a dozen newspapers while she ate it. The difficult part of this job was finished. The next phase was
actually fun. She'd be a new bride in her white dress
and veil, all innocent and wide-eyed.

At dark she undressed and put on a silk kimono that
could be tossed aside in a hurry. She picked up a book
and read until well past midnight, when she heard
Tucker begin to mutter in his sleep and rouse up. The
man must be a horse to take that kind of slug and try to
awake before daybreak. It would never be said that
Katy Hillerman didn't come prepared though. She
opened another capsule and stirred the contents into the
remnants of a cup of cold coffee she'd been drinking.
She draped a towel around his neck and chest and lifted
his head slightly, pouring the coffee down him. Surpris-
ingly, not a drop spilled on the towel.

Tucker went back to sleep like an angel-child. His
dark lashes rested on his face, giving him a boyish
look. Being his wife for a few weeks wouldn't be so
bad; she might enjoy the role. Of course, that doctor
would be one disappointed woman, but then she should
have taken advantage of the situation while she lived

out there on that godforsaken ranch. Katy already had a buyer for the precious Evening Star. An oil man from Houston who intended to use the house for his head-quarters and sink a dozen wells on the land as soon as it was in his name.

Addison slept poorly, awaking several times from nightmares. At dawn she put a note on the door that she'd gone to the Evening Star on a house call and she'd be back by eight o'clock. She bundled up in a heavy coat and started walking. Something was wrong. She could feel it in her bones and it had to do with Tucker. Hopefully, he hadn't fallen and torn the stitches out of his hand, or killed his fool self.

She hadn't gone a quarter of a mile when she met the man he'd hired coming back into town. "Morning, Willie. You already got the chores done out at the ranch?"

"Went out there. Weren't nobody home. Wasn't last night either. I did the chores all by myself last night. Just hooked up the old mule to the wagon since the truck was gone. Tucker didn't answer the door this morning neither. No smoke comin' out of the chimney. Don't know where he took off to. I went ahead and fed the livestock and come back to town."

"Thank you," Addison said. Her breath came out in a fog every time she exhaled. Even through her gloves, her hands were chilled but they couldn't compare with her heart. A coating of ice covered it. Tucker had to be dead. He'd fallen down the steps and broken his neck or there would be fires lit in the house. He should have been up and cooking breakfast. As she stood there, she decided to walk to the next block where the church was located and ask Julius to borrow his car or get him to drive her out to the ranch.

He agreed readily and in a few minutes he, Olivia, and Addison were cramped into the front seat of the automobile. Addison hugged her black bag and fought tears. She'd taken such good care of him to lose him now.

Oh, don't be a ninny. It has nothing to do with taking care of him, but rather caring for him. Admit it. You really have fallen for Tucker. His brashness keeps you on your toes and you've never felt so alive.

"Well, I'll be, there's Tucker's car beside the school. No, it's in front of the house beside the school. Wonder what it's doing there?" Olivia asked.

"Maybe he let that school teacher borrow it since it was raining. Had her take him home and gave her the keys," Julius said.

"She's up to something," Addison said. "Let's go see what it is. Tucker uses that truck for chores and he's not one to loan it out. Willie said he wasn't home last night or this morning."

"You sure?" Olivia asked.

"Of course. She'll be up and around. After all she has to be at school in a couple of hours." Addison opened the car door as soon as it stopped.

Katy had been dozing in a chair to the left of the

door. She heard the car in the driveway, opened the door just slightly, tossed the kimono on the floor beside the bedroom door and swiftly crawled into bed right next to Tucker. She wrapped his arm around her shoulders and snuggled in next to him, pulling the covers up over her bosom, but leaving her shoulders bare. She shut her eyes and waited.

"Katy?" Addison knocked. "You up and around?"

Nothing.

Addison opened the screen door and rapped on the wooden door only to have it swing open. She stuck her head inside and yelled again, "Katy? Did you oversleep? Why is Tucker's truck out here?"

Olivia pushed inside the door and into the living room. "She might be ill. It's her first day for school. She'd be up by now. Katy? Where are you?" She said aloud to Julius and Olivia who were right behind her.

"Mmmmm."

They heard a mumble in the bedroom and tumbled over each other going that way, Julius right behind them. They both stopped so fast that he ran right into Olivia's back, knocking her into the room. The bed stopped her and the jar from her body awakened Tucker, who looked around in a daze.

"Oh, dear," Katy yawned. "Oh, my. Oh, my. This is too embarrassing for words."

"I suppose it is," Julius said stiffly.

"What is going on?" Tucker asked.

"It looks as if maybe you'd better tell us," Addison said.

Tucker suddenly realized he was in bed with Katy Hillerman. "This is not what it looks like." He jumped up and began pulling the covers tighter over his body when he realized he was naked.

Katy began to weep. "Oh, I'm so sorry darlin'. I guess we sampled that bottle of moonshine a little too well and ended up . . . oh, no . . . My reputation is ruined. I'll never be able to teach again. But you said the moonshine was a bottle you'd saved from back when your Granny made it. You said you'd been keeping it for a special day and I should just have a little nip. I'm ruined, Tucker Anderson. Ruined. What are you going to do about this?"

Tucker looked like the only rabbit at a coyote convention. He couldn't run. He couldn't console the woman. He sure hadn't had a drop of moonshine, so what was happening?

"I suppose, Tucker Anderson, that the thing for you to do is make an honest woman out of Miss Hillerman," Julius said tersely. "I'm disappointed in you. I really am, but you will simply have to be a gentleman. We'll be leaving and the three of us will never utter a word of what sin we've seen here this morning. We'll pray for your souls and we'll expect an engagement to be announced by afternoon."

"But I—" Tucker was trapped. He had no choice.

Her reputation might be ruined but the Anderson name had to be protected—for Clara's baby, for Libby, for the children Tilly would have. He'd been hoodwinked but he'd marry the woman.

Addison wanted to beat him to death with her black bag, but he looked so forlorn. Almost like he did the night he awoke from that massive dose of morphine. She narrowed her eyes at Katy, seeing in a moment what had really happened. The woman had drugged him and simply waited. Someone would see the truck eventually and if she didn't show up to teach, then they'd come looking. How convenient that Addison had brought the preacher to witness the abomination.

Chapter Fourteen

Addison fumed the rest of the day. No patients came looking for medical attention, giving her plenty of time to work up an anger that alternately erupted in stomping and then tears. In the middle of the afternoon, Beulah stopped by to tell her about the engagement and Addison unloaded, leaving not a single detail under the robe of discretion.

"And you think he's guilty?" Beulah asked.

"And you don't?" Addison fired right back.

Beulah toyed with the wispy silver gray bun on top of her head, scratching under the hair pins and thinking. "I've known that man since he was born. I ain't sayin' he's been a saint. He's too much like his grandpa for that but there's something fishy going on here. It stinks to high heaven, Addy. That's what I'm sayin' and I don't think he's guilty. I think this new school teacher done saw a ripe plum and picked it off the tree."

Addison remembered the feeling she'd had that something wasn't right even when everything looked like Tucker and Katy were lovebirds caught in a nest. "Really?"

"Be right interesting to see if this is the first time she's stung, wouldn't it?"

"What do you mean?"

"Ever studied the black widow spider? She lures her prey in and then eats him when she's finished with his services. Bet if we had a way of checking, this wouldn't be the first time Katy Hillerman has stung. She reminds me of someone but I can't place the woman. I just feel almighty bad it was Tucker that she set her sights on. Feel bad for him and feel bad for you."

"Why me?" Addison gritted her teeth.

"Honey, things might have taken a while but I had a strong feeling about you and Tucker. You remind me of his grandmother. Don't get me wrong. You don't look a thing like her. She was a quarter Indian and never denied a drop of her heritage. Black hair and eyes just as dark. Tamed Tucker's grandpa to where he was housebroken and almost civil. I thought you might do the same to Tucker."

Addison spit and stammered, trying to find words of denial.

"Oh, don't mind what I think. I might even be

wrong. I'm going to the drug store. Want to join me? We could put a note on the door," Beulah said.

"Wild horses couldn't drag me down to that den of gossip mongers. If there's anything worth hearing, you'll bring it back to me, won't you?"

"Of course I will. When's Tucker coming in for you to take another look at that hand? I swear, he's had his fair share of troubles. But this is the third one. They say they come in three's, you know. First he fell, then he sliced open his hand, and now he's got himself in this predicament. Maybe his bad luck is over."

"He's supposed to be here tomorrow." Addison had already begun to water the seeds of doubt that Beulah had planted in her heart. "You walk slow now. You don't need to be dashing around in that cold wind, and put your scarf on."

"I'm too mean and ornery for a cold to catch me," Beulah laughed as she shut the door. Addison would mull their conversation over and over in her mind. Just in case she didn't take any action, Beulah would begin an immediate investigation on her own. It might be expensive but she didn't want to face Katy Anderson and Bessie in the afterlife and not be able to tell them she'd done all she could. Besides money was only dirty paper with dead president's faces on it, and she had more of it than she could spend in two lifetimes.

Tucker looked sheepish when he propped his hip on the examination table. The gossip vines were smoking since his engagement had been announced Monday afternoon. Several of the church ladies who weren't aware that it was a forced wedding had rallied around her and were offering their services for a reception. She'd refused them all, saying that after the wedding, she and Tucker would host a simple reception in the hotel lobby.

"Let's see that hand," Addison said coolly.

He held it out but didn't look at her. His mind had gone round and round from the time he'd covered himself with the sheet and dressed in the kitchen at Katy's house. He'd told her to plan the wedding and tell him when and where to be; that he'd marry her but it wasn't a marriage of love. She'd laughed in his face and said she'd never love a country bumpkin, but she'd have a big wedding just like she'd always wanted. The ceremony would take place in two weeks.

She didn't tell him but she'd feed enough information to the right people to make everyone believe he was besotted with her. There was no need to deviate from the show. It had brought about results many times and it would this time. She'd brought men with a lot more prestige and money to their graves, and she'd just gotten better each time she worked the scam.

"I noticed Monday morning there was blood on the bandage. What did you do? Fall?" She asked as she unwrapped the bandages to find two stitches broken and the skin around them irritated.

"Addison, I honestly don't know. You sewed me up and it was fine until ... well, you know," he stammered.

"How much do you remember?" She applied ointment and rewrapped the hand.

"I've racked my brain. I left Tilly's to take her home. When we got there she fainted on the front porch so I helped her inside. Laid her on the bed. The place was a mess. Boxes everywhere. Clothing spread out over chairs. The kitchen looked like a hurricane had hit it."

"Oh?" She remembered how neat everything had been when she walked into the house. The woman must have worked all night.

"She said she had these fainting spells often and begged me not to tell the school board. Then she asked me to make her a cup of tea. I did and carried it to her. She wanted me to stay until she felt stronger and asked me to make myself some tea. When I brought it back to the bedroom, I sat down in a chair as far from the bed as I could."

"What happened after you drank the tea?"

"I didn't drink that cup. It was very hot and she wanted it. Said I could have hers. It had gotten lukewarm and she felt better when she had steaming hot tea. So I traded. That's the last thing I remember before I opened my eyes and saw you and Olivia. I want you to know, I didn't take any moonshine in there."

Addison almost laughed. Moonshine was the furthest

thing from her mind and the item that bugged her the least. "I know you didn't. There now, it's all fixed. Anything else today?"

"No. Yes. It's crazy but I've got some strange scratches on me. One on my chest, a couple under my arms."

"Let me see."

He unbuttoned his overalls and undid his shirt and long handles. "Don't know where they came from. They weren't there on Sunday and the ones under my arms really do hurt."

"Fingernails. I'll put salve on them and give you some to take home with you. Tucker, do you want to marry Katy?"

"No, I do not. But I have to. It's the Anderson name. It'd be ruined. I can't do that to Tilly and Clara, or worse yet to their children."

"When is the wedding?"

"She told me the wedding will take place in two weeks. Actually a little less. A week from next Saturday. There'll be an affair at the church and then a reception at the hotel. Vera Holton is making a dress and she's ordering all kinds of flowers and a cake. A big wedding so there can never be any doubt that we're married. I told her I didn't love her and she laughed at me. Said she could never love a country bumpkin but she would have a wedding so her name wouldn't be ruined."

"What did Tilly and Clara say?"

"They're furious. Tilly won't speak to me and says she won't even come to the wedding. Clara is speaking but I wish she wasn't. What she's saying would burn the hair out of Lucifer's nose."

"Can't say as I blame either of them. I was about mad enough to commit homicide myself and I'm not even kin," she said.

"What am I to do?" He asked.

"You're asking me?"

"I guess I know the answer. After a dance, you have to pay the fiddler, don't you?"

"If you dance." Addison looked at him.

"I swear nothing happened." His steely blue eyes begged her to believe him.

"I want you to go home, pack a bag and move in with Clara. Pay Willie to keep up the chores for the next two weeks."

"You've got to be kidding." Tucker raised his voice. "She'll cut me into pieces with that sharp tongue of hers."

"If you're living with Clara, then there can never be a time when you are alone with Katy. That's step one. You are my friend, Tucker—whether I'm yours or not—and friends don't just stand still and let their friends get scammed."

"Friend?" He asked.

"You're a victim, Tucker Anderson. Somehow she knows a lot about you and your family. Like your grandmother running moonshine. No one mentioned that at the dinner and there wouldn't be a reason why folks would tell her something like that. I wouldn't be surprised her name isn't even Katy Hillerman."

"Is moving in with Clara the only option?" He moaned, realizing how stupid he'd been.

"I'm afraid it is. Olivia is here today working on files. I inherited the old doctor's case files along with the cabinets so she's sorting through them. She's got the car so I'll go talk to Clara. Maybe that will help. And I'll see you on Thursday to check that wound again. You've broken two stitches loose and it's red. Open house is in the afternoon from two to five. Come by before that."

"Thanks, Addison, for helping even if it amounts to nothing and for believing me even if it's too late."

"Did it hurt to say that?"

"Not this time," he said.

Addison didn't have patients that afternoon but she was busier than she'd ever been. She and Olivia made a visit to Clara who heard her out and agreed that Tucker could stay there for a couple of weeks. They'd use the excuse of his hand being cut so badly that he needed help. They went to Tilly's who ranted and raved before they could get her to listen to reason. When Addison explained about the scratches and her theory that Katy had had trouble dragging him up onto the bed and undressing him once he was drugged, Tilly was ready to string the woman up by the thumbnails.

Ford came in from the barn before they left and Addison told him what she thought had happened along with

Beulah's story about the black widow. Ford slapped his thigh and shook his head. "A few years ago I read about a woman they called the black widow out in California. She'd married three men and they'd all died within a month afterwards. She inherited a gold mine with one of them and sold it. Seems like another one had a vineyard and I can't remember what the third owned. Each time she'd sell the property and disappear for a while."

"Wonder if Katy is doing that?" Olivia asked.

"If she's that black widow lady, she'd better get ready for a surprise. If one hair on Tucker's head is harmed, I'll plant her sorry carcass in the river," Tilly said.

"We'll be leaving now," Olivia announced. "I've got to be home before supper. Julius is working on his Wednesday night sermon and I want to tell him all this crazy stuff before I start cooking."

Tilly and Ford waved goodbye at the door, then Ford saddled up his big black horse and rode into town. He went straight to the sheriff's office where a telephone had been installed before he'd taken the job as sheriff. Addison might be grasping at straws because she'd fallen for Tucker, but just in case she was right, he had a few legal contacts who could find out exactly who Katy was. Surely it wouldn't be that hard to track down a school teacher and figure out if she'd ever had contact with that black widow woman he'd read about close to ten years before.

* * *

Thursday morning Addison opened the front door to find Tucker sitting in one of the three rocking chairs on the front porch of the hospital. Katy occupied the second one and Beulah the third. No one was speaking but the tension was so thick, it wouldn't have taken something sharper than one of her scalpels to cut it.

"Good morning?" It came out more of a question than a statement.

"Hmpph," Beulah snorted. She grunted when she pushed herself out of the rocking chair. Without a word, she marched into the house and took a chair closest to the fire in the waiting room.

"I'm here about my hand," Tucker said formally. "You said to come by today before the open house party."

"Yes, I did." Addison held the door open.

"And I'm here, darlin', because I need to see my fiancé. His witchy cousin won't let me in the front door." Katy drew her expensive velvet cape around her shoulders and followed Tucker to the examination room.

"You can wait in this room with Beulah. I don't allow anyone in the exam room but the patient."

"Oh, darlin', I am most definitely goin' in there with him," Katy declared.

"Don't call me darlin'. I'm Doctor Carter to you. And don't even try to bully me. If I say you aren't going in that exam room, then you aren't going in there. If you've got a problem with it, trot your little fake southern voice down to the sheriff's office and get a warrant that gives you the right to invade a patient's privacy." Addison bowed up to the woman even if she was a head taller.

"Fake southern voice? What are you talkin' about?" Katy's eyes flashed so much evil that Addison expected fire to begin spewing out of them.

"You're as southern as a Union Army uniform. I went to school with two men from Alabama. You don't have the inflection nearly right. It might fool a bunch of besotted school board members, but it doesn't fool me. I don't care if you talk like a southern belle or bray like a mule. That's your business. But I do have control over my hospital and my patients, and you are not going in there. If you want to talk to Tucker, do it afterwards, and don't be scratching him under the arms again."

"Oh, little girl, you're just jealous because I got him and you didn't. I see that look in your eye. You don't fool me one bit," Katy whispered, the southern accent gone completely from her tone.

Addison slammed the door in her face and turned to face a smiling Tucker, sitting on the end of the exam table. He had picked up her scissors and was carefully removing the bandage from his hand.

"Wipe that grin off your face," she said. Her eyes were nothing more than slits with a slash of green in the middle. Her full mouth was a thin hard line. She crossed her arms over her chest and tapped her toe. The nerve of that hussy, thinking she could give a doctor an order and expect her to jump through hoops to follow it.

"Are you jealous?" He pointed to the door where he figured Katy had an ear plastered to it. She'd shown up on the porch just seconds before Addison opened the door and shot daggers at Beulah with her eyes.

"Of course I am darlin'." Addison raised her voice and put on a southern drawl that put Katy's to shame. "Let me see that hand and then you can go deal with your sweet little petunia. I'm sure she's wanting you to open up your pockets and find all kinds of cash for her fancy wedding."

"Don't you talk about me like that." The door flew open and Katy filled it, her hands propped on her hips.

Using her foot, Addison reached back and kicked it shut again, this time turning the new lock she'd had installed the week before. One thing she'd learned in Little Rock was that there were times in the surgery room when no one needed to come inside. Not for any reason.

She finished the job Tucker had started and put a new bandage on his hand. "Stitches should come out before the wedding. I'd like to see it again on Monday, just to be sure everything is healing right."

"I'd keep them forever if there wasn't a wedding. Addison, I'm scared. I can't do this."

"Then break it off. Clara went to town every day for ten years to wait for a man who said he'd come back and marry her. You think that did the Anderson name any good? And Tilly ran moonshine. What did that do to the Anderson name? Don't be giving me that cock and bull story. If you don't want to marry the woman, tell her no. It'll be the talk of the town for a few weeks and then something else will come along and steal your thunder. In six months, no one will even think about it."

"No respectable woman would ever marry me if I did that," he said.

"You lookin' to get married?" She asked.

"Not right now, but any woman with an ounce of dignity would run a mile to get away from a man who soiled a woman's reputation and then left her practically standing at the altar."

"Your choice. Either way, you'll be miserable. Choose the lesser of two evils and don't look back. Now it's time for you to go face your dragon. That is, if there's a scrap left of her. Beulah might have torn her to shreds. It's like she's messing with Beulah's baby boy."

Tucker's face lit up more than Addison had ever seen it. "Beulah does love me like a grandmother, and if she's got Katy dying on the floor, would you please bring a wooden stake and a sledgehammer?"

"Tucker Anderson!" Addison exclaimed.

"You said you were my friend." He unlocked the door and let himself out.

Beulah marched into the exam room without being called. She sat down on the end of the table and took off her coat. "I'm not here for any illness but to bring you what news I've got in the last couple of days. There was no school teacher by the name of Katy Hillerman in Austin, Texas. Not in the past ten years so she's a fraud. I figure she's heard of the Andersons from one of the oil men around here or someone like that. Did her homework and came up here to do her number on Tucker."

"Is her name really that? Is she out in the waiting room right now?"

"Don't know what her name is. She left in a snit after that little cat fight you two had. I'm proud of you. You stood your ground and didn't let her back you down. That's the way Tucker's grandma would have handled it. Anyway, Tucker is still in the waiting room. I haven't told him I've got someone working on this. No sense in giving him false hope when it might not produce anything. I did give him orders to stay in that room until I came out so he could drive me home. Then I'm going to tell him to go straight back to Clara's and stay there. I don't know what that woman's got up her sleeve. She might fool the men in this town but the women who care about Tucker aren't going to let her get close to him, are we?"

"I should say not," Addison exclaimed.

Beulah slipped her coat back on and left with a smile.

Chapter Fifteen

F*riends?*

Addison could scarcely believe she'd used that word. She arranged cookies on a platter and carried them into the waiting room. Olivia sliced oranges to float in the punch. The curtains were pulled back and light filtered in but the sun hid behind a bank of black clouds. Hopefully it wouldn't rain because Addison wanted the whole town to come out to the grand opening of the Morning Glory Hospital.

Friends?

Her mind jumped tracks from cookies to the hospital to Tucker. He hadn't said she was his friend but had grinned when she said it. When he smiled, her knees went weak and her mind turned to mush. When they passed out common sense, he must have been out chasing

209

butterflies because he sure came up with the short end of the stick. How could he be in the same room with her two minutes not know the extent of her feelings for him?

"Friends!" She muttered under her breath.

"What did you say?" Olivia asked.

"Nothing." Addison looked out the window. Clara, Libby and Briar drove up. She hoped they were hungry and thirsty. They may have to eat a million cookies and drink enough punch to float a fleet.

Tilly and Ford parked behind Clara's car and met up with Dulcie and Beulah walking down the sidewalk. Addison checked the time. Two o'clock on the button. Tucker wasn't with the family and he'd already been in that morning so she didn't really expect him, but disappointment filled her breast all the same.

Those seven had barely gotten inside when a rush of people began to arrive. The street was parked on both sides with cars and buggies. Horses were tied to the hitching rail at the edge of the yard. There was enough noise and talk to fill the house as people wandered from one room to the other. Addison took up residence in the examination room to answer questions. Olivia kept the cookie platters filled and the punch bowl full. Once she'd seen everything, Dulcie ran everyone out of the kitchen, donned one of her old aprons from a hook beside the door and kept the dishes washed.

Addison sat on the table while she waited for the next group to wander through. She caught a moving shadow in her peripheral vision and looked up to see Katy blocking the door.

"Good afternoon," Addison said cordially.

"I'm not here socially," the woman sneered. "I'm here to warn you, Doctor Carter. Stay away from Tucker. I will marry him and I will have that ranch and all his other holdings."

"Oh? Where did you get your information about what he has? I thought marriage was a union between two people so much in love they couldn't live apart. Looks like Tucker is marrying you to keep a blot off his name and you're marrying the Evening Star," Addison said.

"You stay away from him," Katy said threateningly.

"You go have some cookies and punch and enjoy the day. You may need my services some day and I'd want you to feel comfortable here at the Morning Glory Hospital," Addison said as calmly as if she were talking to Tilly. How on earth she kept from picking up a scalpel and removing the woman's make up, was a mystery.

"I'd never let you touch me," Katy hissed.

"I'm sure you wouldn't. Did you know a doctor can tell the age of a woman within a year or two, and I'd guess you are a lot older than twenty-eight," Addison lied.

Katy turned around so fast she practically ran into Clara. She stuck her nose in the air and went straight into the waiting room. She struck up a conversation with several women from town.

"Thought I'd better come rescue you when I saw

who was here. Can you believe the gall of that woman? I swear she's a witch," Clara said.

"She's going to kill Tucker. She's marrying him to get the ranch and his holdings," Addison whispered. Her heart ached. Tears welled up in her eyes but she kept them at bay. She loved Tucker, but there wasn't a thing she could do about it.

Loved Tucker! Friends?

"You look like you've just seen a ghost. And what makes you think she's going to murder Tucker? She's a witch for sure. One that's going to keep Tucker from us, but I can't imagine her killing him."

Love Tucker Anderson!

Addison could scarcely wrap her mind around the idea. He was about to marry the devil's own sister and she'd just discovered that she was in love with him. Clara stared at her as if she'd instantly sprouted horns and a forked tail. She should answer the woman but words were as foreign as ancient Hebrew.

"Are you all right, Addison?" Clara asked.

"I'm fine. It's just scary thinking a woman could be that calculating and cold," Addison's voice came out high and squeaky.

The storm clouds rolled in from the east, reminding Tucker of Katy, who'd come from the same direction and ruined his life. Suddenly, he blinked several times. It was like the day he awoke from the morphine sleep.

Why had he ever thought he had to marry that woman? He'd been suckered and folks would talk but that didn't mean he had to ruin his life for it.

In a few minutes he was in his truck and headed toward town. He'd tell her right then that it was over. She could scream and yell that he was a rogue and a scoundrel until all her black hair turned gray. The fog was lifted from his brain and he wasn't hiding behind a bunch of women any longer. Good Lord, his grandfather would have been embarrassed by his actions. His grandmother would have taken him to the woodshed and worn out a stick of firewood on his hand head for such things.

He fumed all the way to town. He knocked on her door but no one was home. Surely she hadn't gone to the open house after the fiasco that morning when Addison put her in her place. Tucker grinned. Addison was a spitfire when someone crossed her. He missed their spats and he'd like to kiss her again. She'd said she was his friend. He wanted more than that. Not that she'd want him after what she'd witnessed in Katy's bedroom.

He checked the drug store but Katy wasn't there so he went on to the open house. Briar, Ford and Beulah were deep in conversation on the front porch. "Afternoon," he said, tipping his hat.

"Just the man we were about to go see," Ford said.

"I saved you a trip. Is Katy here?"

"Yes, she is. According to Clara she and Addison just had a few more words," Briar said.

"Well, it'll be the last words they have. I don't know where my head has been. Guess I could blame it on whatever drug she loaded me up with, but I don't know that's what it is. I'm not running and hiding anymore, Briar. Thanks for keeping me this week, but I'm going home and I'm going in there and telling her the wedding is off. I don't care what kind of stink it makes."

"No," Beulah said.

"No! I figured you'd be dancing behind me," Tucker said.

"You can't break it off with her just yet. Matter of fact, we want you to keep staying with us and let her keep planning her wedding," Ford said.

"One of you better give me some really good reasons for doing that." Tucker leaned against the post. Through the window, he could see Katy mingling with the four women, describing in detail the dress he supposed since she kept running her hands over the neckline and sleeves of what she wore.

"I've had a private investigator on her all week," Beulah admitted.

"And I made a few inquiries," Ford said.

"What have you found out?" Tucker asked.

"That she may be wanted for murder in more than one state. There's a team of Secret Service men on their way here right now. If you break it off with her she might run."

"Murder?" Tucker felt the color leave his face.

"If she's who we think she might be she's the person who's been labeled the Black Widow. She studies a man's background and his assets and then she swoops in like she did with you. Stuns them. Embarrasses them into marrying her. They die in a few months and she inherits everything they have."

"God Almighty," Tucker gasped. "How'd she find anything out about me? I'm just a common farmer in southern Oklahoma."

"We'll figure that out later. Right now we have to try to keep her here a couple of days. Think you can do it," Ford asked.

"Sure, I can."

"The feds have a couple of witnesses they're rounding up. One in New York. Another in California who know her by sight," Ford said.

"Some sorry fool lived to tell the tale?" Tucker asked.

"No, relatives who were at the wedding and/or the funeral," Briar answered.

"Does Addison know?" Tucker removed his hat and wiped sweat from his brow in spite of the cool weather.

"Addison believed you. She's the one who started all this. We've told her. Made an excuse to tour the exam room while Beulah kept watch on the spider. If Addison hadn't doubted the woman, you'd be pushing up daisies here in a few weeks," Briar said.

"I'm going in and doing my part then. Do I flirt with my fiancé or do I ignore her like I've been doing?"

"Oh, flirt. By all means, be nice. Let her think you've

rethought the situation and you're in agreement with the wedding," Beulah said. "Don't put it on too strong, though, or she'll smell a rat for sure."

"I've never been good at acting." Tucker put his hat back on.

"Haven't you? You acted like you hated Doc long after you figured out you didn't," Beulah said bluntly.

Tucker blushed. "That's another subject. Thanks, all of you. You've quite literally saved my hide."

Beulah went inside with him. "Yes, we did. I'm glad you woke up and stopped the charades, Tucker. You're a grown man who doesn't need to hide from a crazy woman with dollar signs in her eyes."

Katy sashayed across the room and looped her arm in his "Tucker, darlin'. I was afraid you wouldn't make it. Should have known you wouldn't miss something this important."

He placed his hand over hers. "No, I wouldn't. So how are the wedding plans going?"

She stiffened. "I thought you weren't interested in such things. Just tell you when it would be and where to be to save your precious name," she whispered coldly.

"I've changed my mind. If we're to be married then I should be in on the plans. You are a beautiful woman, Katy. I might have courted you for six months and then proposed if we hadn't gotten drunk on moonshine. I'm looking forward to the honeymoon, honey." Maybe God wouldn't strike him dead for lying since it was for a good cause.

"That's right darlin'. Where are you taking me for the honeymoon?"

"The Evening Star. Ain't a prettier place on all the earth. I kind of got spoiled when Doc stayed out there with me for six weeks but I've just gotten back to my routine of running the place. I couldn't go anywhere right now with spring coming and the heifer's about to calve. Doc was already up at the crack of dawn and did the chores alone until I got to where I could get downstairs. I stepped up and helped then but she still drove and honey, she can handle a set of hay hooks like she was born with them in her hands. You ever fed cattle at daybreak and twilight? There could be something right romantic about it. We'd be in the barn all alone with no one but my old dog, Bill, and one lonesome heifer that is waiting for spring so she can get back out in the pasture."

She pushed his hand away from hers and sat primly on a chair. "I didn't figure you to be such a talker."

He plopped down beside her. "Oh, I got lots of plans. Doc showed me how badly I've been needing a helper for a long time out at the farm. You can cook, can't you? With spring right around the corner, I reckon we can put in a big garden and can a couple or three hundred jars of food this summer. Got a heifer that looks like she's going to deliver an elephant or twins. Might need some help pulling a calf since I've got this hurt hand."

If the color on Katy's face hadn't been painted on, it would have drained. She'd take care of the business end of Tucker Anderson long before the garden began to produce, that was for sure. She'd planned to spend the whole summer in Healdton. It was so far back in the sticks no one would come looking for her there. She'd always chosen her marks from big cities where she could fade into the anonymity of the masses, however, the last one in New York had been a little messy. She'd almost gotten caught and barely collected the money from her inherited property before she had to leave the country for a few months.

However, there was no way she was pulling a calf or soiling her hands with a set of hay hooks, either. She'd be the bereaved widow long before that ever happened.

"You didn't answer me?" he said.

"Darlin', you know I'll be happy as a lark at Evening Star even though I've never laid eyes on it. Would you take me out there now to see the place? I bet it needs a woman's touch. Lace curtains and decent China for sure."

"I want it to be a surprise, Katy. You'll be the beautiful bride. I'll carry you over the threshold to your new home and you'll be all aglow with excitement. Whatever you need to make it your home, I will be glad to buy."

"How generous, darlin'," she twittered. He was playing right into her hands. By the time they were married a week, she'd have him signing a will and power of attorney without even looking at the papers which she'd say were bills of sale for lace curtains.

"Would you like a cup of punch?" he asked, wanting

to get away from her. His skin crawled just thinking about the scam.

"No, I've had too much all ready. I think I'll just meander up to the dressmakers and see how that lovely white dress is coming along. Of course, since we've already had a night together, I don't suppose I deserve it, but before that I did. No one in town knows I'm not all innocent and we won't tell, will we?" She nudged his arm playfully.

It took all his will power to keep from flinching. "Would you like me to go with you?"

"Oh, no, not at all. You aren't supposed to see my dress. It's bad luck you know. I'll be busy all of tomorrow, but you might come by my house Saturday if you've a mind to. I expect that wouldn't be too big a sin since we are engaged and all."

"Can't Saturday. Have to do a little work at the farm to get it ready for you. I want everything to be perfect. Would you do me the honor of sitting with me in church on Sunday morning? Maybe we could take a ride afterwards? Over to the Hotel Ardmore and have an ice cream?"

"That's lovely. You can walk me to the door right now and kiss my hand. We wouldn't want the ladies to think we're too brazen so a kiss on the hand will have to do."

Every eye was on the couple as he doted on her all the way to the door and when he brought her fingertips to his lips and brushed a kiss across them, collective sighs from the women could be heard all over the room.

"Stunning performance," Addison whispered at his elbow when Katy was off the porch and prancing down the street.

"I thought perhaps you would show me the examination room and explain just what goes on in there." He turned slowly to face her. "I understand you can actually take out an appendix or operate on a patient on that table. I'm so glad you decided to stay, Doc, and run this hospital. It's a blessing for our little town. So many of the town's folks can't get to Ardmore in an emergency."

"Stunning, hell, it was stellar," she mumbled as she led the way for another one man tour of her surgery room.

"Yes, it is." He kicked the door shut. "Thank you for believing in me. God Almighty, Addison, thank you for saving my life."

"Wow. You are in the wrong profession."

"What?"

"You're so good, you keep your character even when the audience goes home," she said.

"I'm not acting now. I'm telling you the gospel truth. I wasn't even acting out there. I'm a big enough man to admit when I was wrong. You are a damn good doctor and we are lucky to have you. I'll stand on the rooftop and shout it if you want me to."

"That's all right. My ears are still unsure if they're working. Shouting won't help and it'll just make your fiancée angry. We can't stay in here long. There'll be talk. We surely shouldn't have the door shut. Some of those women will run straight to her to tattle." She leaned against the door and made no effort to move.

"You are right." He reached as if to open the door and encircled her with his arms. Steely blue eyes looked deeply into her mossy green ones as he lowered his mouth to kiss her again. Shooting stars filled his head. His heart sang. His soul danced.

"That's not opening the doors." She pulled away and crossed her arms over her chest. Her heart raced. Her pulse wouldn't settle down. What a pickle. She was kissing a man who was for all intents and purposes engaged to another woman. Everything in the world was topsy turvy.

He slung the doors open to find two of Katy's new friends on the other side. "Dr. Carter, that was an amazing education. Thank you for showing me around. Hello, ladies. Are you next in line for the tour. After you see this room, I'm sure you'll be very comfortable bringing your sick folks to the new Morning Glory Hospital. I intend to bring Katy here once we're married. I'm hoping Dr. Carter can help her with those fainting spells she's prone to having."

"Oh, my, I wasn't aware she had the vapors," one lady said.

"Yes, ma'am, she does. I hope she doesn't have one on our wedding day. Wouldn't that be terrible? Of course, even though she's tall, I am strong. I'd catch her if she started to slip away. Don't you think she's going to love the Evening Star and being a farmer's wife?"

"To be sure," the other woman said. "Any woman would enjoy being your wife, Tucker Anderson. I'm surprised you've stayed single this long."

"It is a mystery. Now, you ladies go right on in and ask all kinds of questions." He ushered them in, winked at Addison behind their backs and disappeared.

She hoped the women didn't look closely or they'd see too much color in her face, slightly swollen lips and a grin she was fighting to keep under control.

Chapter Sixteen

Yellow roses entwined with ivy on the wallpaper in Addison's bedroom made her ache for spring. Sunshine poured through the window and if she squinted she could pretend she was outside in the flower garden behind the house at Evening Star. It had been neglected so long it classified more as a bramble mess, but a few days of loving care and it could be coaxed back into beauty.

She dreaded going to church that morning. Tucker did an excellent job of acting, but it wasn't easy seeing him play the besotted fiancé. Hopefully, the whole charade would be finished soon. She kicked the covers off and stretched.

Just because he kissed you don't mean he feels the same about you that you do him. It was a thank you

*kiss. The first one was impulse. The second was the
moment. He was grateful that you'd believed in him
and could see through Katy. You have no right to be
jealous.*

"I know that," she argued with herself. She chose the
better of her two Sunday dresses from the wardrobe, a
dark green wool skirt with a matching jacket with gold
buttons down the front and at the sleeves. She brushed
her hair, parted it in the middle and held it behind her
ears with two gold clasps. When she looked in the mirror, she grimaced. What did Tucker see when he looked
at her? He'd been surrounded his whole life with beautiful women like Clara and Tilly . . . and Katy, who
might be older than she claimed but was truly gorgeous
with all that dark hair and height.

For the first time in her life, Addison wished she was
something more than mediocre. Average height. Average
size. Red hair, which Tucker already made clear that he
hated. Green eyes. Not one thing to mesmerize a man.

Tucker had acknowledged her as a doctor, unless that
was part of the acting job, but many, many times he'd
made it clear that he'd never want a woman in his life
who wasn't docile and willing to do his bidding at all
times. A friendship might be stretching his abilities. It
didn't matter that she'd fallen in love with him.

She had a light breakfast of skillet toasted bread and
hot coffee and watched the hands of the clock move
slowly until it was time to walk to church.

*   *   *

Tucker's eyes popped open after a horrid nightmare. He shut them tightly and felt the other side of the bed then exhaled loudly. It was empty. In the nightmare Katy was back in bed with him and instead of Julius, Olivia and Addison being there when he awoke it was his grandmother and mother. He shuddered. The look on their faces had been one of pure disgust.

"Uncle Tucker, are you awake?" Libby knocked on the door.

"Yes, I am," he called out.

The door swung open and Libby bounded into the room, jumped on the bed and began rattling instantly. "We're going to church and you're going with us and Aunt Tilly is coming and we're having dinner at our house today." She inhaled deeply. "Momma says we can see if Addy can come, too, but Olivia and Julius are going to Granny Roberts' house for dinner. I wanted Olivia to come so I could show her the doll clothes Beulah made for me this week are you going to get up?"

"I might if this little girl would go down to the kitchen and see if Flora has breakfast started. Is that cinnamon rolls I smell?"

"I hope so!" The ball of energy was out the door quicker than a streak of lightning.

Tucker found his dress slacks in the wardrobe along with a pressed white shirt, a clean pair of overalls and a faded shirt. He dressed quickly in his Sunday outfit and ran a comb through his dark hair. His hand itched that morning so it must be healing. He remembered when his leg almost driven him crazy and Addison had brought him the fly swatter.

She'd never be interested in a plain old farmer who wears overalls all week. She deserves a man with a high-powered education. Another doctor who would be able to really talk about all those things she loves. She's so cute with those freckles across her nose and hair that looks like the leaves on a sugar maple in the fall. Any man could fall into those dark green eyes and wallow around in ecstasy for the rest of his life.

"It is cinnamon rolls. Flora said the coffee is ready. Come on Uncle Tucker." Libby didn't knock the second time. She grabbed his hand and led him out of the room.

He listened to her prattle but didn't hear a word she said. He hoped the farce with Katy would be over soon. Acting made him feel very foolish especially in church with Addison sitting in the pew in front of him. His ears turned scarlet at the thought of being so close to Addison and playing court to another woman.

Katy slept until the last minute and then dressed carefully in a light blue wool crepe dress. One she'd brought in case she had to step foot in that classroom. A demure little number she'd ordered from Sears. As soon as she drug out her widow's weeds and black veil, she'd burn the ugly thing. Thank goodness everything had worked in her favor and she'd never have to wear the dowdy store-bought things for very long. The school board had offered to let her teach even after she was married since the other teacher had a husband, but she'd gracefully declined. After all she only had two weeks to get a wedding planned to the most eligible and richest man in Healdton, Oklahoma, and then she'd be helping him run his ranch and take care of his other assets.

She skipped breakfast. Tucker would be taking her to the hotel lobby to eat. The menu was limited, the food barely edible. That didn't matter. They'd be seen as the loving couple right out in public, and that's what she needed. By the time they had Tucker's funeral, she'd have Tilly and Clara eating from her hand. She might even let them have the family dinner at Evening Star. It would be the last time they ever set foot on the property and she'd be gone before the first oil well was sunk.

Eying the shotgun shanty she lived in, she shuddered. It was worth it, she kept telling herself as she went into the kitchen. Faded red rose wall paper covered the walls and the bits and pieces of furniture she'd bought in Austin looked like what she figured a school teacher would own. When she and Tucker were married, she'd either give it away or store it at the farm. From the kitchen she went through the bedroom to the living room and out the front door onto an unpainted wooden porch. She hated Oklahoma. The wind hadn't stopped blowing since she got off the train in Ardmore. It was going to ruin her skin. In her business, she had to look young and desirable. She could act innocent but the complexion did not lie.

Her step was light past the schoolhouse, the general store, the drug store. She scowled when she looked up the street and saw Addison coming toward the church, but that couldn't even drag down her light heart. She'd conquered Tucker in less than a week. He was a puppet and she had the strings in her fingers. Everything was ahead of schedule.

Tucker drove his truck into the church parking area. He smoothed his hair back with the palm of his hand and noticed Addison coming from the direction of the hospital. Rays of sunlight sparkled in her red hair. She looked elegant in a green suit which matched those mossy green eyes perfectly.

He looked the other direction. There was Katy swathed in a blue velvet cape, the hood drawn up over her head. Tucker was reminded of a witch, then he remembered the first time he saw Addison. He'd thought she was a red-haired witch that day but he'd sure changed his mind since then. He looked at Addison and back at Katy. Both walked with confidence and determination. Addison's came with honesty; Katy's with the opposite.

What would he do if she wasn't that woman who'd married all those men and killed them?

I still won't marry her. I don't care if she's innocent as a lamb and this is the first time she's ever pulled a stunt like this. She's not trustworthy and I won't have a woman I can't trust. That would be the same as signing my own death warrant. I can't imagine a life like that.

Ford and Tilly pulled in right behind him. Tilly went inside without looking back or speaking. Ford came to stand beside Tucker.

"They are here. In that black car in front of you are two witnesses and a lawman. Two federal agents are in the one in front of it. The witnesses will identify her and the arrest will be made if she's the woman," he said.

"How will they know with that hood? You can't see her face at all unless she's looking right at you." Tucker kept his voice down.

"Then you better play fiancé again and get her to lower that hood or else they'll come in the church and take her in there," Ford said.

"You really think it's the woman or someone who's copying her?"

"It's time to see." Ford patted him on the shoulder and went inside the church.

Latecomers waved to Tucker, who leaned against his vehicle, waiting patiently for his lady to arrive.

Katy reached him while Addison was still half a block away. She looped her arm through his and kissed him on the cheek. "Good morning, darlin'. Shall we go inside?"

"Of course. You are looking lovely today, but your hair looks different. Did you cut it all off? I hope not. I really like long hair. I can't wait to take all the pins out and run my fingers through it."

She whipped the hood back in one deft movement. "I would never cut my hair, especially now that I know you like it long. See. It's still the same. I'll make you very happy, darlin'."

"Wait a minute. Just let me look at you. I can sneak peeks inside the church, but Granny Anderson said church wasn't where a body went to stare at the women folks. It's where we go to beg forgiveness for all the sins we've committed in the previous weeks." He stopped and looked deeply into her eyes. Nothing there but pure evil.

The door of the first car opened and a man in a black three-piece suit and black fedora stepped out. Tucker could see two women craning their necks and nodding from the back seat. Two men, dressed like the first one, came out of the other black car. All three moved slowly as if they were on their way inside the church. Two were big men and they stopped abruptly in front of Tucker and Katy. The smaller of the three moved into position behind them.

"Ethel Shaw?" One said.

"I'm sorry, sir, this is Katy Hillerman," Tucker said.

"No, this is Ethel Shaw. I'm placing you under arrest for the murder of Marvin Compton," he said.

Katy turned quickly to run but the man behind her slapped a set of hand cuffs on her before she could blink. "It's over Ethel. You had a good run. Ten years and that many husbands. It's time for the killing to stop."

"Tucker, they're lying. I don't know who Ethel Shaw is. I don't know what they're talking about. Get me a lawyer."

"Murder? You killed your husband?"

"Ten of them at least." The man led her toward the car.

She shook off his arm and started running. She hadn't gone twenty feet when she got tangled in the hem of her long cape and sprawled out in front of Addison Carter.

"You tripped me," she said.

"Why would I do that?"

"Come on Ethel. You've been identified. Come peacefully and I won't put the leg irons on until we're in the car." One of the big men pulled her up by the shoulder.

"They're lying. They always hated me. They wanted their father's fortune," she hissed at the women in the car who leaned out and kept nodding to the men.

Addison stood beside Tucker as the cars disappeared.

"That was a little anticlimactic. I expected drawn guns and a big fight. Her screaming and them fighting her to the ground. Not just her running and tumbling over her own feet," she said.

"I'm just glad it's over. Guess we'd best get on inside or Julius will give us those hard looks he saves for those who arrive late." Tucker noticed they were the only ones left on the church lawn.

"You go first. I'll give you time to get settled into the pew and then I'll slip in. If we go in together there'll sure be talk when all this comes out," Addison said.

"Thanks, again," he smiled.

"You are welcome. I'm glad she didn't kill you."

"Me, too." He actually chuckled and left her to wait a few minutes.

She lifted her head and let the sun warm her face. It was over and she was grateful that it had gone off so well. She eased into the seat in front of Tucker and was singing along with the rest of the congregation before they reached the chorus of "Abide With Me."

Julius preached on judging that morning, stating that it was so easy to make a snap verdict and not stop to consider the facts. He mentioned the verse in Matthew where Jesus said, "Judge not, that ye be not judged."

Addison tried to listen but somehow her mind kept going to the Anderson family sitting on the pew behind her. She could actually feel their relief as if she were one of them.

Don't start daydreaming about that, Doc. They're a close knit family and you've been included into their affairs, but you are still an outsider, a drifter. You might have decided to stay on in Healdton but that doesn't make you one of the locals. Not by a long shot. You're still an outsider.

She put the troublesome inner voice out of her mind but she couldn't concentrate on the sermon, either. Olivia would be working at the hospital three afternoons a week with Julius' blessings. That was reason enough to like the man and listen to what he had to say, she reasoned. It didn't work. She wanted to turn around and see if Tucker was still smiling.

Services finally ended and before she could rise,

Olivia was beside her, saying that Granny Roberts had asked them to Sunday dinner and had included Addison in the invitation. "I accepted for you because I was afraid Katy would be here this morning and make Clara feel guilty if she didn't invite her. You sure don't need to have to sit at the same table with that vixen. I wonder where she is. She was supposed to be meeting Tucker and sitting with him. Oh, well, I'm sure he's delighted."

"I'll tell you later. It's a long story," Addison said.

"You can tell it on the way to Granny Roberts' place. They've been wanting to ask you to dinner ever since you healed Granny. She's been spry as a spring chicken ever since you went out there. Said she even made the peach cobbler for today's dinner. I can't make a cobbler worth feeding to the cats," Olivia said.

"Would you like to join us at Clara's for lunch?" Tilly asked when Addison and Olivia reached the front door.

"We're going to Granny Roberts' place," Olivia winked.

"Then maybe next week," Tilly nodded.

"What's the big secret?" Addison asked.

"I'll tell you on the way back after dinner. You've got a story to entertain us on the way and I'll have one for the trip back," Olivia said smugly.

"Does Addison have a ride?" Tucker asked Tilly.

"Guess so, she's going out to the Roberts' farm. They've been trying to arrange a time for her to visit ever since she helped Granny stop dying. Today's the day. Forgot to tell you, Lonny, the oldest son, has his sights set on Addison."

"Great God." Tucker felt as if a big healthy mule had just kicked him in the ribs.

"Yes, He is that," Tilly said without cracking a smile.

"Lonny is just a baby. Not anymore than dry behind the ears."

"He happens to be twenty-three years old. That's not so young, Tucker, and the draft has sent him one of those notices. He'll be going to war soon. He doesn't have time for a long-winded courtship. That's why Granny is so happy to get Addison to say she'll come for dinner. So they can meet and maybe things will work out."

"She's at least five years older than him," Tucker grumbled.

"But she looks so young and who knows? She might go to the war, too."

"She's got a hospital to run."

"Never can tell. Come on. I'll ride with you so you won't feel so all alone. After all you were supposed to have a fiancé to squire around this afternoon. Ford can talk Briar into going with him and Clara will have Libby."

The scowl on Tucker's face practically put out the sun.

Addison sat between two of the Roberts sons. Lonny, the fair-haired, blue-eyed handsome one on one side; Philip, the dark-haired, plainer one on the other.

Olivia, Julius and Granny were across the table from her. Mr. Roberts at the head of the table and his wife, Lizzy, on the other end closest to the kitchen so she could keep the bowls and tea glasses filled.

Talk went to the weather and how they'd enjoyed those two unseasonably warm days, but weren't foolish enough to think spring had really arrived. Winter hadn't been forced into the history pages, yet. There'd be cold weather and to spare before the leaves turned green.

The fact that Lonny would be leaving for boot camp in a week opened up a whole new conversation on the war effort and the hopes that it would be over soon. By the time they'd finished with the weather and the war, Lonny excused himself, explaining that he had a visit to make that afternoon and didn't want to be late.

"He's seeing Maggie Jo," Philip said. "They might even get hitched before he leaves."

"I'm not surprised. They've been flirting for a long time," Lizzy said. "I wish them well."

"Well, nobody told me," Granny said. "I do like Maggie Jo. A sweet girl and a hard working one with good morals. Now tell me why that vixen Tucker is engaged to wasn't in church. And don't be sugar coating it either. I was sitting beside the window and saw those men put handcuffs on her. Did she rob a bank? What happened?"

"I don't know that Tucker wants it told," Olivia said.

"It's not something that can be swept under the rug. It'll be in all the major newspapers. Katy is notorious,"

Julius said. "Might as well be up front and honest about the whole thing."

"Then tell me the story." Granny leaned forward and looked at Addison. "You tell it. You were out there when it happened and you were talking to Tucker after they put her in that car and took her away."

Addison told the tale, leaving out the part about how they'd found Tucker and Katy in bed together. She merely said the woman had drugged Tucker and then convinced him that he'd ruined her reputation while under the influence of moonshine and had to marry her.

"I knew it!" Granny set her thin mouth in a firm line, creating even more wrinkles around her twinkling eyes. "Us women ain't so easy fooled as you men. Philip, you take note here. Always out chasing some skirt tail from another town. Pick you out somebody close to home who we know all about. Like Maggie Jo."

"Yes, ma'am." Philip actually shuddered. "She really killed those men after she married them? For their money?"

"Looks that way," Julius said.

"Okay, now that we've got the air cleared around that, I want to know about Tucker's hand. What's happened to it? One time he's got the bandage on the right hand and now the left. Can't he remember which one is hurt?" Granny giggled like a school girl.

"The right one is healed pretty well. The left one got sliced open with his pocket knife when he was opening a bag of feed," Addison said.

"You're going to have to marry that man to keep him out of bankruptcy, much as he's running up doctor bills." Granny slapped her leg in glee.

"He doesn't like red haired women. He doesn't like short haired women. He sure doesn't like women who are doctors and we'd kill each other the first week."

"Just like Katy Hawk and that Anderson man she married. Never can remember his first name. Mean as a snake even if he was a handsome feller, but Katy tamed him down pretty fast. Some men just take longer to soften up. They have to stay in the hot water a long time. Others see the error of their ways pretty quick and learn to say, 'yes, dear' early on. Tucker Anderson will have to boil a long time."

"You surely have that right," Addison agreed, uncomfortable with the whole conversation, especially since she'd just recently realized she had feelings for the man.

"The woman who sets her sights on him better have a good strong backbone and a sassy tongue. That man'd walk all over a sweet little whimpering woman," Granny said.

"Now, Mother, that's enough badgering Doc about Tucker. She might not even like the man," her son said.

"Pshawww. We'll see. Now tell me about Beulah. Is she faring well? I worried about her when Bessie died. Thought we'd surely bury her in the next week. Guess me and her are both cut of tougher old bull hide than that. We will both end up outlasting time. The rapture will have to come and take us away. We're too tetchy to die."

"That might be blaspheming," Philip said.

"Could be, but I'm old and God overlooks the senile," Granny guffawed.

Addison wondered how big of a pot of boiling water it would take to fit Tucker Anderson into and if the recipe would say to cook him for a lifetime?

Chapter Seventeen

On Monday morning the headlines in the morning paper were a full inch tall. "HEALDTON MAN IN-STRUMENTAL IN FOILING BLACK WIDOW." The article stated that Tucker Anderson was a hero because he'd worked with federal and local authorities in help-ing bring the infamous Black Widow, a woman who lured men into her net and then killed them for their money, to justice. It listed all the men she'd married in the past and stated that Tucker had been her next victim until he'd realized who she was and informed the law of her whereabouts.

Tucker read it twice. He'd been billed as a hero in-stead of a sucker. He wondered who he should thank? Addison had been the one who set the ball rolling but there was Beulah with her investigator who was still on the case trying to figure out who had given Katy/Ethel the scoop on his assets and Ford who'd had an inside track with law enforcement. At least his neighbors and friends wouldn't snicker behind his back. Instead they'd be patting him on it.

He sighed and laid the paper on the breakfast table. Hero. Sucker. It didn't matter. Addison wouldn't be able to resist Lonny Roberts. He was young and good-looking and he hadn't stood on a soap box and shouted loudly about how he'd never let his heart control his good sense by marrying a woman with a career.

Tucker took his heavy heart out the back door to do the morning chores. He didn't see the beautiful sunrise, didn't stop to scratch Bill's ears. He went to the barn to feed and water the heifer and calf. Soon the grass would be green and the weather nice enough to turn them both outside. The calf would romp and play, free as a bird. Tucker sighed again. His heart was cooped up like the calf. It yearned to be free and run through the fields with Addison.

He moved the cow and calf into an adjoining stall where there was fresh hay and water, then rolled the wheelbarrow in place. He picked up the scoop shovel and began cleaning the stall, not paying a bit of attention to Bill when his old tail began wagging and he ambled toward the barn door.

"Did you see the morning paper?" she asked.

He jumped. "What are you doing here?"

She'd looked like a picture from a catalog the day

before at church. All that dark green the same color as her eyes, but that morning she appealed to him even more. She wore a pair of faded overalls, a plaid flannel shirt and her red hair was tucked up under a stained old hat that had seen better days.

"Came to visit and see my calf like I said I was going to do. Olivia and Julius were going to Ardmore for some kind of early morning breakfast with the ministers of the county so they dropped me off at the end of the lane. You didn't answer my question."

"I saw the paper. Where's Lonny?" he asked bluntly.

"Why would I know where Lonny is? I guess he's with Maggie Jo. That's who he's seeing. Or else he's home helping his father or getting ready to go to the service," Addison said.

Tucker could have bit his tongue off. Now he had to explain. There was no way around it. Might as well be up front and honest, get it over with. "I heard he had a crush on you and that's why Granny Roberts wanted you to come to dinner yesterday."

"And that made you jealous?" She raised an eyebrow.

"No, of course not." He picked up a scoop shovel and went back to work.

"My calf has doubled in size. I bet he could be turned out to run next week. Did the heifer have her twins yet or was it just one? You haven't been out to feed this morning have you?"

"It's my calf and I was already planning to turn him out in a few days so I don't need you telling me what to do. The heifer hadn't calved as of last night and no, I haven't been to feed."

"Good, I'll bring the truck around and help you, and Tucker, be careful with that hand. Stitches come out in a few days but you could do some major damage mucking out stalls. I'd hate to have people saying I brought you back from the dead just to kill you with infection."

"You didn't bring me back from the dead. Katy or Ethel or whoever she is didn't get a chance to kill me."

"Wasn't talking about Katy. I was talking about you falling off the roof. That's what gave me my halo and angel wings in town. I saved the almighty Anderson and kept him alive for six weeks without killing him."

So he was jealous about Lonny. Olivia had told her on the way home that they'd thought Lonny was sweet on her and Granny was all for the match, but it had fallen through right after dinner when he announced he was going into town to see Maggie Jo.

Tucker is jealous! Tucker is jealous! She sing-songed in her heart.

That meant somewhere deep inside his heart he liked her whether he was ready to admit it or not. She wanted to dance a jig in the pig trough right beside the barn door. Instead she fired up the truck and brought it around to the barn doors, grabbed a pair of hay hooks and loaded the truck bed full. By the time she finished, Tucker had the stall cleaned, fresh hay on the floor and ready for another day.

"You drivin' or you want me to?"

"I can drive," he grumbled.

You've been given another chance with this woman and you're about to blow it to the devil, too. What do you want, Tucker Anderson? A silver-plated invitation to court her. Maybe a sign? Like the finger of God burning a big heart on the oak tree down at the school playground that says Tucker loves Addison. Love! I don't love this woman. I don't hate her anymore and I think she's a fine doctor. But love her! I don't think so. I'd have to eat crow pie and wash it down with pride if I married someone like her, who had a career and had no intentions of giving it up. And that's where love leads . . . straight to the altar.

"Why are you scowling? Have a bad night?" Addison was so glad to be back at Evening Star she could scarcely sit still in the truck seat. She wanted to bounce around like Libby when she was excited with new kittens or puppies. She'd missed the smell of winter in the air when she did the chores. Missed the dog. Missed the calf. Missed Tucker. All of it and she didn't care who knew.

"I'm not scowling and I had a wonderful night," he lied.

Ruin it. Ruin it. Why don't you just throw her out and tell her to walk home.

"Then wake up and enjoy the beautiful morning. I love mornings. Can't see why anyone would lay abed when there's a sun coming up and things to do. Waste of time and energy if you ask me," she said.

"Well, would you look at that?" He grinned as he stopped the truck beside the pasture fence.

The transformation made her gasp. Tucker was handsome with any expression on his face but when he smiled her world stood still and her breath fairly well left her body. She looked in the direction he pointed and there was the young heifer and two wobbly little calves still wet, trying out their legs and having breakfast at their mother's udder.

"Guess she did it all on her own," Addison whispered. "Aren't they beautiful?"

"Why are you whispering?" He asked.

"Because God is right here. He's in this lovely morning. He's hovering about those gorgeous babies. It'd be a sin to talk out loud in His presence." She opened the door and grabbed the hooks. "By the way, where's Willie this morning?"

"I gave him the day off. His wife wanted to go to Wilson to a cousin's wedding. I figured I could do the chores with one hand even if it took me a while."

When the truck was empty, they both leaned on the fence and stared at the new baby calves. "Looks like your streak of bad luck is over," she said finally.

"What makes you say that?" he asked.

"Look around you. You are alive. You've got a lovely ranch. This year's calf crop has started out with double luck, triple if you count the one in the barn," she said.

"I hope so."

Speak up or forever hold your peace. It wasn't Lonny but that don't mean there won't be another young man who'll see the prospects.

"Addison, I'd like to court you but I'm not very good at it," he said bluntly.

"What makes you think you're not good at courting?"

"To begin with, I'm past thirty and never did much of it. Gathering wildflowers and bringing a woman candy seems so foreign to me."

"You enjoying this moment?" Her heart was beating so hard it was about to bust the bib pocket right off her overalls.

"Of course I am. Well, mostly, I am. Have to admit, I'm nervous about saying I want to court you," he said.

"Not all courtin' involves candy and bouquets of flowers, Tucker. That's nice, all right, but this is, too. And if this is the way two people want to court, then who's to say you're not good at it." She slipped her hand in his.

"Seems strange. Courtin' isn't supposed to be workin'." He liked the way her hand fit so well in his.

"Depends on what a body calls workin'. See, to me this isn't work. It's fun." She closed the distance between them until they were shoulder to shoulder.

"Runnin' a ranch isn't work?" He asked.

"Not if you enjoy doing it. Success is enjoying what you do. If you don't like your life, then it's miserable."

"Think there could ever come a time when you could run the hospital and help run the Evening Star both?" He didn't look at her. He didn't want to see her face when she turned him down.

"Yes, I do. Think there could ever come a time when you'd be willing to let me do both and not grumble about my job?"

"I think so."

"That's not what you've said before." She looked up to see smoldering steely blue eyes declaring more than his words.

"I've fallen in love with you. I guess we're supposed to court some more before I tell you that, but I have."

"Me, too." She wrapped her arms around his neck and drew his lips to hers for another icy hot kiss that set her nerves on edge and turned her legs to jelly. If this was courting, she couldn't take a lot of it.

"So after we court for a while, do you want a big wedding or do you want to slip away quietly like Clara and Briar did and like Tilly and Ford?" He kept his arms around her, holding her close to his heart.

"Oh, Tucker, I want the whole works. I want the dress, the cake and my father and brother to be here. I want a reception in the Hotel Ardmore and the whole town of Healdton invited."

"How long do you think we'll have to throw hay and watch the sun come up before that happens?"

"A month." She kissed him again.

He groaned.

"Two weeks?" She teased.

He grinned.

She kissed him again.

"One week and the wedding and reception can be right here at the Evening Star. I'll love the courting but I want to be a wife. I want to wake up in your arms in the morning. I want to see all the baby calves when they're newborns. I want enough kids to fill up those bedrooms upstairs."

"We'll fight," he hugged her tighter.

"You can count on it. I'll expect lots of kisses to make up when we do."

"You can count on it," he whispered in her ear. Then he gave her another long, lingering passionate kiss to seal the deal.